A CIRCLE OF STONES

A CIRCLE OF STONES

Shelagh Macdonald

ANDRE DEUTSCH

First published April 1973 by
André Deutsch Limited
105 Great Russell Street London WC1
Second Impression May 1982

Copyright © 1973 by Shelagh Macdonald
Printed in Great Britain by
Robert Hartnoll Ltd. Bodmin, Cornwall

ISBN 0 233-96406-1

First published in the United States of America in 1982
Library of Congress No. 82-70629

for Gilbert
as well as all the kids

Serifos. An island
rock
keeping secrets
glinting beneath olive trees

Pitted stone glares
dips into green
bowls hiding wine-fruit

Crystalline Serifos
remembering Perseus
fleeting with star time
through then
through now

A circle of stones seals the story.

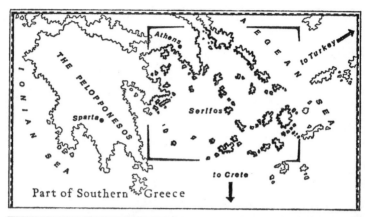

Part of Southern Greece

some of the Greek Islands
Enlarged from above

I

'Here? English people? Coming *here*? To live?' Pethi leaned all over the table.

Zoë smoothed honey on to paper-thin pastry. 'The pink house is let' – shoving her son's hands away from the chopped nuts – 'Aspassia told me.'

'But ... *here*.' It was unheard of. 'Maybe it's just for a holiday.' Pethi walked to the open door to stare up the rocky hillside to where the village concentrated itself in bright cubic heaps. The pink cube was the nearest house to their own, its faded shutters peeling, secret. 'When?'

Zoë said nothing. Pethi, still gazing up the hill, knew she had shrugged. 'Well – what *else* did Aspassia say?' It was intensely irritating, his mother's calm at this astonishing news. Aspassia, the most enthusiastic talker they knew, would have been buzzing with it, for certain. So would all the village.

'That's all.'

Pethi crouched in the doorway to stroke Vleppo's black fur, hot in the spring sun. The cat's yellow eyes blinked in slits, a large paw stretched and spread. He too was unsurprised. Pethi shook him slightly, to impress him. 'Here, on Serifos. Of all places.' The cat pulled back his paw, settled, and went back to sleep.

* * *

She held her small brother's hand and leaned on the steamer's rail. The bare hulk of the island glided by, a distance away yet, as they steered for the harbour mouth. The girl stared.

Then, the boat's wake curved. There it was. The harbour, the village.

She turned. 'Dad?'

'We're here then.' Her father stood beside her.

'Dad. Have I ever been here before? Ever?'

'Never.'

'Not even when very small, even then?'

'No. When we came here, you weren't born.'

'That feeling. You know. As we came round – those houses up there, the village on the peak – as if I'd seen it.'

'That's where we're going.' Her father rested a hand round her shoulders. 'Lots of other Greek islands have a similar look. I dare say that's why it seems familiar.'

They stood watching the island draw near.

'It's rocky,' she said. 'Bare.'

'A ring of mountains, a circle of stones,' said her father. 'Once, they say, it was all green plains.' He grinned. 'Remember the myths?'

* * *

'They've arrived? What d'you mean, they've arrived?' Pethi more or less fell off the donkey, bringing a pannier with him. 'How do you know?' Only days had passed since they had first heard: things just didn't happen that fast on the island.

Zoë snorted a laugh. 'Everyone knows.' Rubbing a hand through her son's crazy hair. 'Aspassia just went up there.' She nodded at the pink house. 'She heard they want someone to help. She said they're from London – ' tethering the donkey, 'did you get everything?'

'London!' The house glowed in the sun.

'They came on the noon boat from Piraeus.'

Pethi groaned, slapping his head. 'Just this once I didn't meet it . . .'

'Everyone else did', Zoë mocked him, carrying the pannier through the blue doorway and dumping it on the table. She called: 'It's a man with two children. He's tall, wears glasses – '

'Two? Two – English – children?' Pethi was all disbelief.

'I imagine so. If he's English, and they're his children . . .'

'The mother?' Pethi leaned at the door, his long limbs making angles.

'There doesn't seem to be one. Nobody's asked yet.'

'There must have *been* a mother.'

'Oh, quite. That's logical.' Zoë grinned.

'But then . . .' to himself, as he moved into the sun again, 'not everybody has a father, either.'

He squatted on the stones beside Vleppo. Characteristically the black cat jumped on to his shoulders and purred into an ear, deafeningly. Then settled leggily round the boy's neck. Pethi's eyes were fixed still on the pink house.

A London family. In there now. Now. Usually, the pink house was empty, except in high summer when an Athens doctor and his family arrived to escape the city's heat. These English must have rented the house from him. Why should English people, London people, do that? Serifos wasn't fashionable. When foreign visitors came, if they came at all, it was usually on shiny tourist steamers. They stayed in the hotel by the harbour and in a day or two were gone again, to more glamorous islands.

Pethi listened to the minute sounds of Serifos. A whisper of wind in the silver olive leaves, the goat muttering behind the house, a stone shifting under the donkey's hoof, the purr of his cat. Up the hill, a small child called. That was all. Pethi had an idea that to a London ear these sounds would add up to silence. Why, some Serifiots themselves complained the island had nothing. Pethi smiled a little. Even they did not know. So how could these strangers, these people from London, guess the secret of his island? Pethi's own secret.

Then came the noise he hoped for: the clunk of a plate put down firmly on the wooden table indoors. He twisted round to watch the doorway.

In seconds Zoë was there, a scarf round her dark hair. In one hand a plate piled with nut-and-honey pastries, oozing sweetly. Pethi grinned. Zoë licked the honey off a thumb, looked up the hillside, and said 'Come on', then strode up the rocky steps.

Pethi, with the fur collar of Vleppo still clinging, leapt after her.

He was in for some shocks.

First, his mother began to speak English the minute they were beckoned indoors by the smiling, bespectacled man. Pethi gave him hardly a glance for his amazement and outrage at Zoë.

'You never told me – ' he hissed as they were shown into a cool room half-filled with spilling packing cases.

'You never asked,' Zoë replied blithely, infuriatingly.

The man, who said he was called George, spoke English back at her. Pethi was livid. He could hardly catch a word;

English lessons in the one island school had been few and desultory. The man George told Zoë he was Scottish, not exactly English, although the language was almost the same. He and Zoë laughed at this. Pethi looked blank as his mother explained the joke: he had heard that the British had the curious habit of humour. Sideways he observed the unusually tall, strange man with pale skin and hornrimmed glasses, brown hair greying near the ears. He might be nice enough, in a not especially handsome way.

His second shock was Tini coming suddenly into the room. Pethi was so rigid with disbelief at the sight of George's daughter that Vleppo stopped purring and dug his claws subtly through the boy's shirt.

Pethi knew something of beauty. He knew his island's beautiful places, and it was common knowledge that his mother was beautiful, in a proud, elegant way, with gleaming dark hair and wide near-black eyes; the same colouring as Pethi himself. But Tini was something unknown. Tini shone. Her skin reflected pale light in the shaded room. Her hair was so fair it was silvered, in straight shimmering strands. Her eyes were big and bright, flashing an extraordinary blue, the sea in summer. Tini was a vision, even dressed in a creased shirt and jeans.

George was introducing her. 'How do you do?' Pethi got out, clutching at an English phrase. It nearly finished him when she replied with '*Kaliméra*', the Greek 'good day', and walked towards him holding out a hand. Her smile was more of a provocative grin. She shook hands with Zoë too.

'You speak Greek!' Pethi cried.

'My mother was half Greek,' Tini explained, sitting

gracefully on a packing case. Glancing at her father – 'He speaks Greek too, only far better than I can.'

Pethi smirked at his mother. George said, this time in Greek: 'Your mother's English was so good, I was lazy'. And Zoë smirked back at Pethi. Then remembered her manners.

'We brought you these.' She held out the pastries formally. 'To welcome you to our island of Serifos, and wish you happiness here in Greece.'

'Oh!' Tini's nose was practically on the plate. 'Thank you. Aren't they what you call *baklavá*?' Pethi and Zoë nodded.

'We'll all have coffee,' said George, taking the plate with thanks and skilfully removing Tini's fingers at the same time. 'Which Tini will kindly make. Now.' Turning to Zoë and Pethi – 'You will, won't you, stay and have some coffee?' His Greek was indeed very good. 'Sit down – er – here' – he moved some boxes, uncovered a chair or two. 'Sorry about all this. Get a move on, Tini.' She was in the doorway to the kitchen, watching Pethi. To his amazement, she beckoned to him as she disappeared.

Pethi, with Vleppo still attached, followed.

'You can talk to me,' she said, 'while I make coffee.'

Pethi fidgeted bare feet on the stone floor, feeling dumb and stupid. Tini filled a kettle, turned and smiled.

'What's his name?' Nodding at the cat.

'Vleppo.'

'Vleppo? That's the same as "I see", isn't it?'

'Yes. Vleppo sees everything.' Pethi didn't smile at Tini's amusement. 'He is, in fact, the most intelligent individual I know, and he and I always know what the other is thinking.'

It was a reproach. Tini's grin was a shade less mocking.

14

'Oh.' Rattling the kettle on the stove. 'And does he always sit round your shoulders like that?'

'Often. When he wants to look at people straight instead of craning up from the ground.'

'Ah. Well, that does seem intelligent.' Briskly she sorted out cups, checking for dust. 'And – I hope you don't mind my asking – ?'

'Mind?' Pethi considered the shine of her hair. 'Greeks ask plenty of questions themselves, you'll find.'

'Well, then. Vleppo has got – hasn't he? – rather large feet for a cat? I noticed.'

'Certainly he has,' Pethi agreed. 'See, he's got an extra two toes on each foot, rather like thumbs. They're called super-numerary digits, or so our *pappas* tells me, and he knows about animals. *Pappas* is "priest" in English,' he added courteously.

'Well, they seem fine feet to me.'

'He's an excellent rock-climber.'

'I can imagine. And does he really know what you're thinking?' Vleppo's moon-yellow eyes looked straight back at her.

'Oh yes.'

She reached to stroke Vleppo's wise black head. He pushed his nose against her hand and purred, a fine imitation of a motor boat.

'He likes me!' her blue eyes dazzled. 'Doesn't he?'

It occurred to Pethi rather late that he had been holding forth pompously about his cat instead of talking about Tini.

'I could've told you that,' he said.

'Oh?' She laughed. Pethi laughed too, with a sudden relaxed happiness to be with this new friend.

And the kettle boiled.

George was answering Zoë's questions. 'I write books,' he explained. 'Oh good, coffee.' He took the tray from Tini and poured four cups.

Zoë was impressed. 'Novels, you mean?'

'So far, one novel and a book about Greek myths. But that's why we're here. So I can write more. It's impossible in London. Costs too much to live there, and I couldn't afford to write all the time. Had to be a bank manager to survive.'

Zoë and Pethi stared at him. 'You mean, you gave up a job as a bank manager to come here, to Serifos, to write?'

'For good?' Pethi asked.

'Uhuh,' George nodded. 'Probably for good. Depending.'

'Well,' said Zoë, gazing at her coffee.

'But Serifos? Why Serifos?' Pethi asked.

'Liked it when I first saw it, years ago.'

'This isn't one of the popular islands . . .'

'Very true,' said George. 'But it's what we want.'

'Come on, Dad,' said Tini. 'There's a bit more to it than that.'

They looked at her. George grinned.

'Dad's also a fanatic about archaeology.'

George looked modest. 'Something I've studied in my spare time.'

'He's got letters after his name,' Tini said more specifically.

Zoë laughed. 'Well! Sorry, but you really have come to the wrong place. The only things anyone ever dug for here were metals – iron, all that. And hardly any of the mines are any good now, they say.'

Pethi could no longer fight a rising anger. 'Archaeologists don't come *here*,' he scowled. Nobody noticed.

'Dad has a theory,' Tini revealed. 'It all began when he was working on the myths book, along with some other ideas he dug up.'

George hid his face behind his coffee cup. 'We'll see. I may be wrong.'

Pethi burst out aggressively. 'You wouldn't come all this way, throw up your job, if you thought you were wrong.' Zoë turned to him in surprise.

George nodded slightly.

Pethi laughed, almost contemptuously. 'Classical remains? Is that what you mean? Here? Surely you don't think we've got a Parthenon or something on Serifos?'

'Pethi!' cried Zoë. 'You are rude. Remember that in Greece a stranger is our guest.' Pethi ignored her.

George was unruffled. 'All right, Pethi, suppose I'm on to something. Yes, you've got a point when you say I think I am. Suppose I found something like that. Say . . . a temple to the goddess Athene, like the Parthenon even. What would happen?'

Pethi was pale. Then he shrugged carelessly, as if to dismiss the whole ridiculous idea. Zoë reached out a hand and shook him impatiently.

'Serifos would be discovered, people would come here. That is what would happen, foolish child.'

Pethi's lips trembled with anger. 'So? Who wants people coming here? I like the island the way it is.'

'Bah!' cried Zoë. 'You don't think. And you are impolite.'

17

Pethi was outraged. '*You* like Serifos too!'

'*I* like it, yes. But you ask Mrs Vassiliadis, and Mrs Panayiotis, and –'

'Oh, all right, all right!' His hostile shoulders made Vleppo jump to the floor.

There was silence. Then Zoë breathed deeply, calm again, and apologized to George.

'These women I mentioned,' she explained, 'their husbands and sons have all had to leave the island because there is so little work. Every month men leave Serifos, and the population is dropping. Some go to Athens, which isn't so bad, but others go to Australia, America –'

'I know,' George nodded.

Pethi rounded on his mother again. 'But the alternative, eh?' he snapped. 'Think of the things you've always said yourself about the islands which have been ruined. Juke-boxes and high prices, and the food in the tavernas not so good –'

'But Pethi –' Tini cried, 'that sort of thing is up to you. The Serifiots. Not every popular island is spoiled. If more people came here, you'd all be more prosperous, and families wouldn't be broken up. You'd be able to sell more of the things you make – the rugs, the knitting – and shops could be opened, and more cafés, and boats could be hired, and rooms let –'

'It could be wonderful,' Zoë clasped her hands.

Pethi looked fixedly at his feet. Vleppo leaned against the boy's legs and stared out of the window. George felt sorry, seeing Pethi's unhappiness, that he'd mentioned his dream of Athene's temple at all. He shifted in his chair.

'Anyway,' he said, 'it would all take ages. The explorations alone. And chances are nothing will be found. Ever.'

'But,' said Zoë, 'it just might.'

'It just might,' agreed Tini.

Pethi said nothing, hating them. But then everyone looked towards the door where stood Jason, swaying, plump, smiling, three years old. Zoë leapt up and snatched him into her arms with instant love, and Tini explained he was her brother, rather eccentric, that he already spoke a few words of Greek, and she wondered how he had slipped away from Aspassia, the Serifos woman who was going to help them in the house. ('My kindest and closest friend,' Zoë told her.)

In the general hubbub, Pethi dealt with his black mood, at least superficially, and managed his parting words almost pleasantly.

'What was wrong?' Zoë looked at the back of Pethi's neck, thin beneath the mop of black hair, as they went down the slope.

'You mean apart from calling me a foolish child?'

Zoë giggled. 'Oh that. You know it meant nothing.'

'And apart from not telling me you spoke English?'

'Oh yes. Well, sorry Pethi. It never occurred to me. That all?'

'No, it's not all.'

'What then? You've always said before it'd be a good thing if we had more visitors to the island. What was it?' Zoë's kind hand went to her son's shoulder. He shook it off and turned off the path.

'See you later,' he mumbled. Zoë watched him jump over some rocks and walk in the direction of the cliffs. Vleppo stalked beside him like a conspirator.

2

'Why was he so annoyed, that Pethi?' Tini wondered.

'Speak Greek,' said her father. 'No English unless you're exhausted, until you're fluent.'

'Tyrant,' commented Tini, Greekly.

'I imagine,' said George, tearing open another box and pulling out heaps of plates, 'he can't bear the idea of tourists all over the place. You can't blame him. I dare say many others would feel the same, in spite of the advantages.' He cursed as he dropped a saucer which broke.

'Speak Greek,' said his daughter smugly. She helped him pick up the pieces. 'No,' she said. 'I don't think that was it. Not entirely. Besides, as far as I can tell the islanders love visitors. Look how everyone greeted us when we arrived – and Aspassia's being marvellous, working much harder than she need. I think something else was bothering him.'

'Well, I dare say you'll find out,' smiled George. 'But meantime go and give Aspassia a hand with Jason, or the beds. Or both.'

*　　*　　*

'Aren't they nice, Aspassia? Pethi, and Zoë. And Vleppo.'

Aspassia's brown face was live with pleasure above a pile of sheets. A lean face, and somehow noble, with deep lines about the mouth and eyes. Thick greying hair was fixed in a bun. She smiled crooked teeth. 'Zoë is very dear,' she said. She dropped the sheets on a bed, rolled her dark eyes, clasped her hands. 'She is so good, so sweet.'

Tini turned over piles of blankets. 'How I'd love to look like that. Tall, elegant, dark . . .'

'Oh yes?' Aspassia's bright eyes mocked. She tossed a sheet towards Tini. It billowed over the bed. 'If you have a nature half as nice as Zoë's, people will put up with your looks,' she said. Then scowled, and wrenched the sheet viciously to tuck it in. 'Nevertheless. There are those who would be bad to her, to my dear Zoë.'

'Oh no!' Tini encouraged. 'Surely nobody could be bad to Zoë.'

'Aaaah! Holy virgin mother!' Aspassia cried. 'You think not? Ha!' She pounded a pillow unnecessarily hard. 'You will in time no doubt meet my brother-in-law, the fiendish Thanos. And then perhaps you shall see how a man can be bad, my little flower.'

'Thanos?'

'Yes indeed. The brother of my good husband, and none who know them can believe they have the same blood in their veins. That wicked Thanos.' She made a swift sign with her hand towards the window, presumably in the direction of the wicked Thanos since Tini took it to be a sign of ill will. 'He protests that he loves my Zoë, but his love is not a good love. It is a love that takes. That wants to own.'

'Thanos loves Zoë?'

'So he has said for many years. Bah.' Aspassia abandoned the bed-making, sitting on the half-arranged blankets to talk. Tini joined her. 'Thanos, he wants Zoë.' She looked bead-eyed into Tini's face to see that she understood. 'It drives him mad, crazy, that she says no to him.'

'Why? I mean, why does it drive him mad?'

'Because once, years ago when she first came to Serifos, not much more than a child and with her beautiful child Pethi not yet born, he seemed kind to her, and she was grateful, and polite. And he hoped that she might love him some day.' Aspassia's brown knobby hands twisted and flapped as she talked. 'And then, some things happened here on the island. Things that Thanos was responsible for. Bad things. And Zoë realized his kindness was shallow, and worth little. Soon she made it clear that she didn't like him, didn't want him to see her. Then he was angry. His pride was angry.'

Aspassia was speaking fast, and Tini had trouble keeping up with the language, forced to interrupt from time to time to gather a meaning.

'And Zoë came here before Pethi was born . . . ?'

'Ah! What a tale!' Aspassia cried. 'But of course you haven't heard it yet. She was shipwrecked, when her beautiful Petros had gone . . .'

'Petros?' It dawned on Tini. 'He was Pethi's father?' Her confusion wasn't helped by Jason rummaging in a cupboard. She hauled him out and gave him an old newspaper to demolish. 'Go on,' she said to Aspassia.

'Oh yes. A fine and strong and handsome man was that Petros. Zoë has shown me his picture.' To Tini's fascination, tears began to roll down Aspassia's sunburned cheeks. 'He was washed overboard, drowned, never seen again.'

Tini sat down again, appalled.

'It was her father's fault, all of it,' wailed Aspassia, wringing her hands, rocking slightly. 'They were so in love, the young couple, and her father would not let them marry. No, he said. This fisherman is not good enough for my fine daughter Zoë who is educated and will marry a rich man of my choosing. Such a creature as this moneyless Petros, he said, will create bad, inferior grandchildren for me, children I will not want to inherit my lands –' Aspassia waved a hand, indicating distance, in what Tini took to be roughly a western direction, '– for Zoë's father is rich, if he lives still, and owns a great deal of property away on the Peloponnesos. Ah, that too was a foolish and wicked man, the father of Zoë.'

Tini waited while Aspassia rocked to and fro a little, her hands over her face. Gently she asked: 'And what happened?'

'He locked her up, so she shouldn't see Petros. A thing to do! This lovely young girl, who loved Petros so much. But still, they planned. Zoë's uncle helped them. Petros borrowed money, and bribed Zoë's maids. And they ran away together, the beautiful couple. Her uncle let them hide in a tiny cottage on his land, by the shore, where Petros could finish preparing the boat he had built for them. They decided to sail round the Peloponnesos and be happy together somewhere on the west side where Petros' cousins lived. Ah, they were so happy, they were to make a wonderful life. Her father, he couldn't find them. Ah, they were so happy . . .' She stopped to wring her hands and moan.

'And then . . . ?'

'They set sail. They went. But a storm spoiled it all. A terrible storm which came suddenly, as sometimes they can. It broke the mast of the boat, and the rigging, and as the brave

23

and handsome Petros tried to drag in the sails, a wave took him. Snatched him up, and threw him over the side. And Zoë saw him – his face turned to her, his arms reaching out – but she could do nothing, nothing. She tried to catch him, but he was gone, into the darkness. Gone.'

Aspassia's voice was low now. 'Zoë, she didn't care if she died. She left the wheel of the boat, and crawled into the cabin. The boat was thrown about by the storm. She hoped it would dash against the rocks, somewhere. She wanted to sink to the bottom of the sea, with her beloved Petros, for no people ever loved so much. She thinks she fell asleep or was unconscious, she didn't know for how long. When she woke up the sea was calm and the sun hot. She felt weak and ill, not having eaten, maybe for days. Perhaps she had gone a little mad. She found some of the food they had brought, and ate. Then she came more to herself and remembered her Petros being taken from her by the sea, and began to cry. She kept crying, she said for a day and a night. Just crying.'

There was silence in the little bedroom except for the sound of Jason tearing newspaper.

'Then, as dawn broke, it was my husband Dimitrios who saw the poor broken boat.'

'Your husband?'

'Dimitrios is a fisherman, with his own fine fleet of boats, although no thanks to that evil-thinking brother of his. He was returning from the night's work. There was Zoë's boat, almost upon the rocks of Serifos. He thought it was empty, but no! Poor child. She was only in her teens, and so pale and thin, so ill, weeping all the time, calling for Petros. Dimitrios thought she had lost her mind. But he brought her home, poor child, poor little bird, and we took care of her. And Thanos helped. In those days Thanos hadn't shown how bad he could be. He was arrogant, and selfish, but . . . as I say, he had money, and he took a fancy to her, for she was beautiful as she grew well, as you can see for yourself today. Dimitrios and I – we love her, she is a daughter. Their little white house there, down the hill, it was part of my dowry. Now it is Zoë's. We gave it.' Aspassia's sigh was long. 'That was fifteen years ago and more.'

Tini's voice croaked. 'And Pethi?'

Aspassia smiled again, at last, and rested strong hands on her flat front. 'He was here,' she nodded. 'Within Zoë. Petros had given her this beautiful child – a better grandchild than Zoë's father ever deserved.'

3

The back of Pethi's neck was guiltily aware of Zoë's gaze until he reached the top of the rocks. Then he dropped out of her sight, shrugging with the relief of it. Ahead of him was a low, craggy cliff. At once, he changed direction. Instead of heading for the way down to the small white beach below, as Zoë had supposed, he turned at right-angles to cut off a narrow cape of the island and make for another part of the coastline.

The detour took him past the edge of the village, over the ridge where the row of windmills whirred. Wild flowers shone among the rocks and green leaves of shallow valleys, swinging and nodding as Pethi's bare brown feet moved firmly on. On another day, setting off on this walk, Pethi's whole body would have been filled with joy and aliveness, responding to the colour of the rocks and flowers and sky. He would have stopped occasionally to look about him, to stare into a bright flower, to talk to Vleppo, and in general to act with the happy freedom of solitude and a glorious secret.

But today he was screwed into a scowl, hunched with resentment. Anger made him kick at the ground, made him tremble. And fear. Astonished, he realized he was afraid. Something which he loved and valued was threatened. And at the same time, he was ashamed.

Vleppo walked immediately behind Pethi, plodding steadily

on his large feet. He felt the mood. He didn't bound ahead to pounce on invisible intruders behind the rocks, twitching his whiskers in the clear air. Instead, as Pethi's gaze was fixed frowning on the ground about a metre ahead of him, so Vleppo's was fixed somewhere near Pethi's heels. Only if a remark was addressed to him did he turn his lamp eyes up for a second or two.

They walked a long way. Over another ridge, into a valley. Up a hill, a narrow goat-path between rocks. Across the old, dry river bed. But now, Pethi's eyes lifted and brightened. He ran up a short slope, leapt some stones, and stopped abruptly at the edge of a high sheer cliff, to fling out his arms in a gesture of welcome at the view.

The coastline here was mass upon mass of rock, turned and lifted and heaved about by ancient earthquakes, long before man. The strata rose and fell in waves, twisting and curving, sometimes split into great crevices. The drop below Pethi and Vleppo was enormous, ending in a petrified jungle of jagged rocks and the sea of turquoise glass. This cliff was one side of a giant cleft which cut back narrowly into the island's coastline. Facing them was the other side of the cleft, another dizzy cliff: it glowed redly in the afternoon sun. And it was to this opposite cliff that Pethi's glance flew. About halfway down its perpendicular face, dark in the sunlit rock, was a cave mouth. 'There it is again, Vleppo,' he murmured. Below the cave the cliff fell away, apparently smoothly, to reach the jagged rocks far below. It looked totally inaccessible.

'Ready, Vleppo?' Pethi said, and stepped over the cliff.

His feet were at once on a ledge, his chin level with the clifftop. Vleppo walked neatly on to Pethi's shoulders, settled, and waited. Without fear or hesitation, the boy moved down the rock face. His feet and hands found holds swiftly and lightly: the way was so familiar now he suspected he could find it with his eyes shut, or in the dark.

At first, he moved straight down the cliff. Then diagonally and to the right. From above, the cliff-face was deceptive, seeming sheer and unbroken, but in fact there were plenty of firm holds and crevices. Pethi now moved vertically down the cliff again, until he reached a ledge, which he followed to the right and gradually downwards. The ledge broadened more and more, finally opening out into a natural, wide platform – a thick tongue of rock stratum. It was here that the two sides of the great cleft almost met: the two cliffs reached out towards one another. For the opposite cliff, where the cave was, also formed a platform, almost identical in shape. It spread out, broad and strong, towards the one where Pethi stood. Between the two platforms was a gap of less than half a metre – a mere step across.

Above Pethi and Vleppo the cliff bulged, overhanging them: it was impossible to see the platforms from the clifftop they had left. Below them was a terrifying drop to teeth of stone. Pethi didn't even think of it, let alone glance down. He crossed from one side of the platform to the other with as much ease as he might have crossed his own doorstep.

The cave was now out of sight, hidden round a bend, behind a rocky outcrop on the cliff, but on the same level as the platforms. This second platform too led into a ledge which ran round the cliff, the edge of a stratum of rock. Pethi moved surely along the ledge, easily finding hand-holds. Round the craggy bulge of cliff he edged. And there was the cave mouth, a few metres away. 'There it is,' Pethi whispered, 'Vleppo, there it is . . .' The ledge ran right below the cave, and in seconds Pethi was standing with his shoulders on a level with the cave floor.

Vleppo stepped confidently into the cave, and Pethi swung himself after. He was here again, in his cave. His. As he gazed enthralled into its blackness, his dark mood flew off into the bright afternoon. This was where the magic began, the magic that was his own, for nobody else to discover or share. Except Vleppo, who understood.

Vleppo had become invisible. Pethi found his small torch in his jeans' pocket: the cat's eyes were brilliant in its beam. 'Lead on, Vleppo. You're the one who sees.'

The cave floor was flat for only a short way, perhaps five or six metres, and then the floor sloped steeply downwards, a tunnel running deep into the cliff. The sides and floor were quite smooth, and in parts the slope was too steep to walk down directly. Pethi had to negotiate his way with hands, feet and bottom. The first time they had come here it had been difficult and frightening: what would be at the end? Where did this strange cave lead? But now Pethi was sure of the descent, and Vleppo made no false steps.

Down down down. After about five minutes the slope eased, becoming almost level again. Then, the tunnel opened out, becoming a great, dark cavern. Silence hung here. Pethi shone his torch round, marvelling again. Rocks shimmered crystalline and red, purple, blue and green. Along one side, a curtain of stalactites made a brilliant, frozen waterfall. The cavern roof soared out of view, out of reach of a torch beam.

Pethi swung the light round. 'Vleppo?' A blurrp from the cat led Pethi on, and now his torch lit a natural archway, a door out of the cave, almost concealed by the end of the stalactites. He followed Vleppo through it, into a short passageway, almost a porch. At once this opened into another cavern, smaller than the first. It was circular, and here the colours in the rocks were lit subtly by an indirect glow, so that Pethi could see without a torch. High above, daylight was seeping in, presumably from somewhere among the rocky wastes of the clifftops. Pethi had never found from where. The cave roof near one side narrowed into a kind of rocky chimney, leading up and up, out of sight. Light fell down this chimney from rockface to rockface, filtering through ferns, arriving finally in Pethi's secret cave as a mysterious twilight.

It took him by surprise, every time, the feeling of this place. Each time he left, he told himself it could have been no more than his imagination, or perhaps some unusual feeling of happiness. Each time he returned he expected that it wouldn't happen again. But now, as he stood, his face lit palely by the cave's glow, it began again.

First, the peacefulness. The air was full of peace, breathing peace. And then, gradually, the feeling of power. It was as if he grew taller here, stronger. As if he could do anything at all, in the world, in the universe. As if his feet had wings that might take him soaring through unknown places and dreams. He couldn't understand why it happened. He only knew it must have to do with her, the secret of his cave, the secret that he and Vleppo had found.

On his strangely light, strong, winged feet, he crossed the cave to the place where daylight shone most intensely. And dropped to his knees. On the cave floor, the light gleamed on palest marble.

'Here she is, Vleppo,' he murmured. 'Athene.'

An owl called high above them.

4

'Nobody,' stated Pethi, 'swims as well as I do.' Twisting away fishlike among the rocks.

'Oh,' Tini replied inadequately, her hair spread to dry in the sun. Vleppo watched the vivid water inscrutably.

With a swirl and a shower of diamonds Pethi surfaced, clutching a silver wriggling thing in one hand. 'See?' he yelled, all exuberance, 'a fish for Vleppo!' The cat's whiskers angled forward like antennae.

'How did you do that?' Tini was amazed, watching Vleppo pounce on his meal and start to devour it.

Pethi's eyes slid sideways. 'As I said.' Shaking his shaggy wet hair. 'I swim better than . . . you, for instance.'

'That's true.'

'You're not arguing?'

'No.'

He kicked at the sand. 'You don't mind?' Staring down at her. Against the blue of the sky he looked particularly brown and thin.

'No. Why should I?' Tini believed in things rational.

Pethi gazed at the green water between the rocks. 'I do like to do things best,' he admitted finally.

'You're in luck. You *do* do things best.' Such indifference.

There was silence except for the miniscule sound of Tini

scratching one long golden leg, and slight gnawing noises from the cat. Then the sand crunched near Tini's head, and Pethi had run and plunged into the sea again. She opened her eyes, raised her head, and watched him dive and surface, splash and cavort, like nothing so much as a mad dolphin.

In just a week, Tini thought, one could see that Pethi was someone different. Not just different from the boys she'd met at school in Notting Hill: that was predictable enough. But different too from the boys on Serifos. The ones that had been on the beach with them that morning – Nikos and Stavros. Pethi's friends. They had been uncomplicated, frank, and somehow more physical. They asked curious questions, directly. In comparison, Pethi had remoteness. He seemed somehow older.

The boys knew it too, Tini realized. She lifted an arm to study its increasing tan, the bleached hairs contrasting with the gold skin. Beyond her arm she could see Pethi's dark head, a distance from the shore; he swam strongly.

Yes, Nikos and Stavros seemed almost to be wary of him. He had a subtle distancing effect, even though they all laughed together, playing wildly in the water, leaping over rocks. Yet, the boys appeared to respect him, to value his opinion. She had the feeling they wouldn't mock him privately, even though she sensed they thought him strange to keep a pet cat. She had seen them looking sideways at Vleppo. Well, it was odd, admittedly. Even in England it would look odd, a boy being followed everywhere by a large black cat with oversized feet. She giggled to herself. But here on Serifos, it was odder. Nobody seemed to keep pets.

Or perhaps it wasn't Pethi who kept his friends at arm's length, but the other way around. Because he had no father?

Tini realized that on this small island in a limited society some people might disapprove of Pethi, the son of an unmarried woman. But no, not the boys. They had sought him out, as if it were an honour to be his friends. And Pethi? He didn't seem to be concerned if the boys of the island wanted his company or not. While he had still been at school they had been playmates. But no one boy was his close friend. Pethi's best friends were men – like Dimitrios, Aspassia's husband, and Tassos, whose café they'd decided to visit today. And she had the feeling he liked her father too, despite that first antagonistic reaction about the archaeology. But apart from them, Vleppo was his friend. Just the same, she reflected, Pethi did seem to like her company.

Tini felt suddenly flattered, and sat up to comb her hair out of its silvery tangles.

'Sometimes I'm not polite.'

'What?' She jumped.

Pethi had emerged, all droplets, and stood beside her. His words had the ring of a confession. Tini had to search back to discover where their conversation had ended.

'See how rude I was to my mother the day you arrived.' He thumped his bottom down on to the sand. 'I was angry with her that she spoke English and hadn't told me, and she could have taught me better than I learned at school. Still, I could have been polite.'

Tini decided against saying she had thought his anger had been about something else. 'Oh, poof,' she said. 'You're allowed to be annoyed sometimes, surely. If you were "best" at being polite as well as everything else you'd be boring. Anyway, I could teach you English.'

'You? A girl?'

Tini stopped combing her hair. 'Your mother's a girl. Isn't she?'

'That's different.'

'Oh?' Tini was between mocking laughter and irritation.

'Also,' Pethi didn't notice her change of mood, 'I was rude to your father and to yourself, and for that I apologize.' He was overwhelmingly formal.

'Oh, nonsense.' A mixture of sympathy and her previous annoyance made her go on. 'I can understand your feelings perfectly. Perfectly. Naturally enough you wouldn't want people coming here, finding out –'

The reaction was an explosion, Pethi on his feet.

'Finding out?' His face all fury. 'What do you mean by that?'

She had gone too far. 'I'm sorry. I was only saying I understood –'

'No!' Pethi's feet danced in rage. 'You were not! You were saying – "I know something" – you were prying –'

'Oh, rubbish!' She lapsed crossly into English.

He bellowed at her. 'How do you know? How do you know?'

Tini looked up at Pethi, marvelling at the Greek temper. His dark eyes flashing sparks, his hair standing out black and wild, he was extraordinarily handsome. Still, she had been stupid. She stood up with smooth grace. 'Pethi,' she said, quite quietly. 'I have to explain that sometimes I *do* just sense things. Not that I'd completely realized I had, this time. I don't know how it happens, but –'

'HA!' Pethi's back was to her.

'But,' firmly, 'if you have a secret, I don't want to know it, see? I don't want to.' He didn't move. 'In fact,' she clinched it, 'if you tried to tell me anything right now I should refuse to listen.' She picked up her shirt and dragged it on. Pethi turned.

'You don't want to know?'

'No.'

'Not even if you think I've got a secret?'

'Not bothered. Not in the least.'

'Oh.' Pethi cast a rock into the sea.

'All I should have said was – I didn't blame you being angry the other day. And I'm sorry if I seemed to be nosey. I suppose I was prying. A bit. I was irritated that – oh, never mind.'

'Oh, well.' Pethi spoke from inside his shirt.

When he emerged, she smiled at him. 'Come on. You said we'd go down to Tassos' and have an ice-cream.'

As they climbed the steep rocks away from the white little beach, Pethi said casually: 'I think you swim quite well, too. Considering.'

Through the donkey-cart width of village streets, where houses leaned, Dimitrios pounced.

'Where've you been all week?' were Pethi's first words after introducing Tini.

Dimitrios grinned. He was a small man, like many of the Serifiots. Pethi was already very slightly taller. Dimitrios' face was sharp: the chin, the nose, the cheekbones all clearly defined. Lines ran deeply down his cheeks, emphasized by dark grey stubble. He always seemed to need a shave. His smile was wide, flashing white and gold, and his eyes were, of course, dark, with a shine of excitement. He ignored Pethi's question, clutching affectionately at the boy's hair with a rough brown hand.

'He is a good boy, this one.'

'Yes,' Tini found his grin infectious. 'I'm pleased to meet you at last Dimitrios. Your wife Aspassia's already a friend –'

'Ach, that Aspassia woman, she talks a great deal.' He rolled his eyes good-humouredly. 'Going down to Tassos? He's been asking for you.'

'Yes – coming?'

'*Po, po, po, po!*' Dimitrios made the Greek noises of disapproval, unconvincingly. '*I* cannot linger over ice-creams and coffee. I must work. Although –' he bowed his curly dark head gallantly – 'I would dearly love to buy an ice-cream for our beautiful new Serifiot. Eh, off you go' – giving Pethi a shove – 'and you be a gentleman.'

Laughing they parted. Ten paces away Dimitrios called back: 'Eh, Pethi! Take a look at your boat while you're down.'

Pethi spun about, his face bright. Dimitrios, with a mischievous wave, was round a corner and away. Pethi stood as if fixed while Tini and Vleppo stared at him. And then, with a look in his eyes that couldn't be assessed, he turned back again. Without speaking, he hurried on the way they had been going, towards the mule track which joined the winding road down to the harbour village. His companions followed. Tini for some reason felt she should ask no questions.

'The heat!' Tini gasped, her eyes screwed against the dazzle of the harbour. 'Why is it so much hotter down here? I noticed it when we arrived on the boat. And it's not even summer yet . . .' She flapped her shirt to circulate some air.

'It's enclosed,' Pethi explained briskly, evidently feeling nothing, striding energetically even after the long walk. 'An oven, they call it. At the height of summer it's often unbearable, so still and hot. That's why people built the village at the top as well, I suppose.' The upper village of Serifos that they had left was now a glistening heap of sugar cubes up on the hillside.

'Have we really walked six kilometres? Where's Tassos' café? Oh, for an ice-cream.' Tini dragged her feet.

'Back there . . .' Pethi waved a vague arm. Then stopped, realizing. 'Do you mind? I mean, if I first –'

'The boat?'

He nodded, very serious. Tini let herself be led round the curve of harbour, dawdling through the occasional shade of a tamarisk tree.

'What boat is it?' she asked once, but Pethi said nothing. She wasn't even sure if he had heard.

Nets were drying near bright fishing boats pulled up on shallow beaches. Agile brown fingers mended, piercing eyes looked up under weathered blue caps, friendly voices called. One man washed sponges, squatting behind a large bowl of darkening water. On one side of the bowl was a pile of almost black, squashy big blobs. On the other side after the washing, a softly-glowing pile of beautiful yellow sponges. It was a miracle. But Tini couldn't linger without losing Pethi, who had his own miracle in mind.

At last, off the end of the stone-paved quay, a small wooden jetty. Here rocked a row of brilliantly-painted fishing boats, and some caiques. Pethi stopped. 'Dimitrios' boats,' was all he said, and seemed stuck in his tracks.

The nearest boat was newly painted in red and yellow, so

38

glossy it looked wet. The colours repeated in the water, a gently-moving mirror. After a few seconds Tini realized that it was on this boat that Pethi's stare was fixed. She looked at him: he was solemn, and . . . strange. She looked back at the boat. It was certainly beautiful, even to someone whose main experience of sailing was watching dinghies on the Thames. But this boat was quite large, with the romantic curving shape of a caique, but sleeker, more slender. It had a slim, high mast, and a second, shorter one. Indeed yes, it was beautiful. Brass ringed the portholes of the cabin. The ropes were clean and white, neatly coiled. But why this effect on Pethi?

And then Tini, following idly the gleaming curve of the bows, and waiting for enlightenment, saw. Painted in neat Greek lettering: 'Πετρος'. Petros. Of course.

Pethi was moving forward, perhaps dazedly, his hand reaching out. Tini's mouth, opened to announce what she had realized, shut again. She edged away along the jetty to look with concentrated interest at the other boats, at the sea, and anything else that happened to be around. Vleppo stayed close by Pethi.

All that Pethi could think was: 'It is mine. It is mine. At last, it is mine.' He even murmured the words aloud, in wonder. Such pride, and happiness, and some sadness somewhere too. It was inexpressible.

It was all of five minutes before he called Tini.

'See, Tini,' his hand making a trembling flourish, 'she is my boat.' Tears in the eyes didn't seem to embarrass a joyful Greek.

'Yours? You mean – all yours?'

'My own.'

'It's beautiful.' She waited.

'It was my father's.'

'Petros.'

'Dimitrios has kept it in good condition all these years. He said when I was old enough he'd equip it again for me. For me. And he has.'

'Oh, Pethi. No wonder you didn't see him for a week.'

'It has sails. And an engine too.'

'And you – you can sail it? On your own?'

He nodded. 'Of course. Dimitrios has always taught me the laws of the sea.' His hand caressed the mooring rope. 'If you wish,' and Tini knew she had been honoured, 'you may help a little.'

'Oh. Oh – Pethi – when?'

'Soon.'

'You'll have to teach me.'

With a peremptory kind of miaow, Vleppo suddenly leapt aboard the *Petros*, then turned his black face and yellow eyes to Pethi. It was what Pethi needed to break his sense of awe, of hardly daring to touch his beautiful new craft.

'Yes,' he said, 'let's look at her.' He sprang on to the forward deck, and yanked Tini after him.

The small deck area was painted white, the cabin shone with brown-gold varnish. Everything reflected sunshine. Inside the cabin were two bunks, fat with red cushions. A tiny cooker was fixed against one side.

'Hey, look at this!' Tini was more fascinated by the ship's cooking arrangements than she would ever have been in the kitchen at home. 'These pans are made so they fix – look – they can't slip off the cooker if the boat rolls.'

At the end of the cabin was another tiny compartment, with a small lavatory that flushed with astonishing vigour. 'Most houses on Serifos don't have such luxury,' remarked Pethi.

They admired the wheel, and the brass housings of the compass. They peered under the sail covers and found that the *Petros'* sails were red. They fingered the tiny, gleaming rails, and stared through the port-holes. Pethi was speechless, running his hands over everything.

'Had you never been on board before – I mean, even before it was repaired?'

'No, never. It was in Dimitrios' shack where he works on his boats. I'd seen it often enough, but not like this.' Pethi leaned on the wheel and gazed up the length of the mast. His boat. The boat his father had set sail in, for a life of happiness.

Tini watched him, wondering what he thought, seeing his face solemn, perhaps sad. But he turned to her and grinned.

'Dimitrios was right,' he said. 'You *are* beautiful, and you deserve that ice-cream.'

Vleppo ran ahead towards the café.

Tassos, a tall, handsome, moustached, iron-haired Serifiot, welcomed the two young customers with loud warmth and announced that he would bring them his speciality. He disappeared, singing.

They sat at a round dented metal table under a tattered umbrella. Pethi sat on one chair, placed his feet on second and third chairs, and angled his arm on the back of a fourth. Tini sniggered.

'In Greece,' informed Pethi, who had come across her attitude among foreigners before, 'there are always four or five times as many chairs in a café as people. So you can relax.'

'You Greeks aren't rational,' said Tini, 'but it seems a good idea just the same.' She spread herself likewise. 'I suppose that's why so many of the men play with worry-beads too, to relax their nerves. I used to think they were a kind of rosary for praying.'

Several of the men dotted about the café tables, talking, drinking coffee, reading newspapers, swung these small bright strings of beads in their roughened hands.

'*Komboloi*, they're called,' said Pethi. 'Maybe many centuries ago they were for praying. And I suppose you could say that relaxing your nerves is a kind of praying.' He felt rather pleased with that remark, in spite of Tini's derisive snort. In fact, he thought, wriggling his toes in the sun, he felt pleased with everything.

The ice-cream arrived, a wondrous thing of six different flavours, a fruit sauce poured over the lot. Tassos was beaming with achievement, and presented Vleppo with a dish of goat's milk. As Tini rapidly saw, this was a favour indeed for a cat. Within seconds a circle of about twenty other cats had gathered at a safe distance from the lapping Vleppo. 'Pethi – look . . .'

Pethi nodded. 'They're everywhere.'

Compared with the sleek Vleppo, these cats were a pathetic sight. Their eyes and ears were huge in comparison with thin, wild faces. Their fur was stark, with lumps pulled out, their bodies horribly skinny. They were like demons, but demons full of fear, creeping near then jumping in terrified retreat at any quick movement.

'Oh, poor things. Can't we give them some milk?'

42

Pethi ate his ice-cream. 'They live on rats and mice and scraps.'

'Who owns them?'

'Nobody.'

'You don't care!' She stared at the ring of haunted eyes.

'Oh yes, I care.' Pethi looked at Tini. 'Listen,' he said. 'First of all, hardly anybody can afford to keep cats as pets here. People can hardly feed themselves.' He saw her glance at Vleppo. 'Oh yes, Vleppo's an exception, but he's rare in Greece. But that's because I – well, for certain reasons, I undertook to look after him, personally. His food is my own responsibility.' Tini remembered the silver fish. 'So cats are here, all over the place, because they breed fast. They're useful to the island because they catch vermin. People take no notice of them.'

'But they look half-starved!'

'Yes, they are. They get ill, too, or they fight to the death. And lots of kittens are born dead – probably just as well.'

'Can't anybody do anything? At least do something to stop them breeding so fast. A few cats would catch just as many mice and rats, and they'd get more to eat.' Tini was upset.

'Yes, something could be done, but most people aren't interested. You can't blame them.' Pethi looked defensive on behalf of his island. 'Visitors from rich countries never understand. But when you're as poor as some Greeks the only animals that matter are the ones that work, like donkeys and goats. And a few dogs.'

'But the cats work. They catch things. You said so yourself.'

'It's not the same.'

'Why? That's not reasonable!'

43

Pethi smiled at her. 'You'd better meet the *pappas*. He has some scheme in mind for dealing with it. I dare say he'd welcome a helper.'

'The *pappas*? Well, why didn't you say so?' She dug into her ice-cream. 'The *pappas*! Why him, anyway?'

'Well, it sounds peculiar, but before he went into the church he did various other things, including being a veterinary surgeon.'

Tini laughed. 'I don't believe it.'

'It's true. Anyway, he has some plan to get equipment from Athens, chloroform and heaven knows what, so that he can put down any cats that are injured, or ill, or deformed, or whatever they happen to be. Also he'll "doctor" tom kittens so that the breeding rate is cut down.' Pethi nodded towards Vleppo. 'Like he did for Vleppo – that's why he doesn't go rampaging about with the other cats.'

At that moment Vleppo left his dish of goat's milk and sat under Pethi's chair to wash his face. As he moved, the stray cats leapt forward to finish the last drops, spitting horribly at each other in competition.

'Poor souls,' Tini said. 'There are so many.' She paused. 'I'll help the *pappas*,' she resolved. 'It's a very reasonable plan.'

Pethi grinned. 'You like things to be reasonable.'

'Of course.'

They watched the cats. 'Don't you think,' said Pethi suddenly, 'that sometimes things just *can't* be reasonable? I mean, mysterious. Inexplicable.'

'Supernatural, d'you mean?'

'Maybe. Yes.'

44

'Well, I suppose so. At any rate, things can be mysterious and inexplicable. But that doesn't mean they're not reasonable, does it? I mean, there must *be* a reason, even if we don't know it. It's only reasonable!' She grinned.

Pethi thought of his cave. 'Well,' he said, 'eat your ice-cream. That's a reasonable thing to do on a warm day.'

Tini was exclaiming deliriously over the next exquisite cool flavour when a burst of angry shouting rose from a table at the back, near the cafe doors, in deep shade. A group of men that they hadn't noticed were sitting there. Pethi's head shot up, his lips a line. Vleppo crouched, ears flattening. The stray cats sprang away and disappeared.

'What is it?' Tini's question was ignored.

A man, dark, neither tall nor short, broke away from the shadowed group to walk rapidly between the café tables. He seemed athletic, quite powerful, although dressed in a sleek suit. He shouted harshly over his shoulder at the men he had left. Two men sprang up from the table and shouted after him; one of them spat.

The man walked briskly towards Pethi and Tini, not seeing them, swinging a string of expensive-looking amber *kombolói* on a gold chain, with short angry movements. Not until he was right next to the table did he see Pethi. Then, to Tini's alarm, he stopped. His scowl was directed at Pethi now, who looked back at the man expressionlessly. Fear shivered in the warm air.

'Ha!' said the man loudly, injecting the word with a sense of threat. Tini was suddenly aware that Vleppo, under Pethi's chair and near the man's foot, was swearing and spitting viciously. The man heard him too, and looked down. For a

45

brief moment he looked as if he might kick the animal. But instead he sneered, and walked away quickly.

Tini saw that her hands were trembling. Pethi was slightly flushed. The argument at the men's table was louder now, and being joined by men from all over the café.

'Thanos?' asked Tini, she hoped casually.

'You knew?'

'I guessed. Aspassia told me about him. About him and Zoë, and about your father Petros and the sad story.'

'Ah yes.' Pethi licked his ice-cream spoon. The bright day had changed a little. He leaned over to stroke Vleppo's angry fur. 'Thanos is an evil-thinking man.'

'That's what Aspassia said.'

'For all she talks a lot, Aspassia's no fool.'

'Vleppo swore at him. At Thanos.'

'He always does. Vleppo has reason to hate Thanos too.'

'Thanos was afraid of him.'

'Afraid?' Pethi snorted. 'Of a cat? Not him. How can you say that?'

'I just felt it. Why did he stop like that?'

Pethis shrugged. 'He deceives himself that my mother would have married him but for me. Pah.'

The noise continued at the table in the shade. Other men still joined the group, and everyone talked at once. Fists banged the table, and glasses rattled.

'What's it about? They're talking too fast for me.'

'About the mines.'

'On Serifos?'

'Yes, the iron mines. Most of the men working in the mines work for Thanos – the men from these two villages, that is.

46

He's the manager. It's a bit more complicated than that, though, because he owns most of the land where the mines are. His father and grandfather owned it before him – that's Dimitrios' father and grandfather too, of course.'

'So why are the men angry with him?'

'He keeps sacking the men, saying there isn't enough work in the mines. About ten men were sacked last month – most of them have had to leave the island to get more work – and there are rumours he's going to sack some more. Not only that, but he keeps reducing the wages of the men that are left.'

'But that's not fair.'

Pethi's smile was wry. 'No indeed. That's what Spiros and Giorgos think too – ' he indicated the table of talking men ' – especially as they think they will be out of work soon. But they were arguing with Thanos because they say it is worth doing some more investigating to find if one of the mines could be extended. They say that for all anyone knows it could still be rich. Thanos said no, that it would cost too much to bring in equipment, and as he was certain they would find nothing he would lose money. He also said that the Mining Company – the controlling company – in Athens have refused to put up the money for such an idea.'

'But if there's a controlling company, surely they're the people who are authorizing the sackings and reducing the wages?'

Pethi shrugged. 'That's what Thanos says.'

'And it isn't true?'

'It might be. But nobody trusts Thanos.'

'Then why don't the men check with the Mining Company? Why don't they find out?'

'It wouldn't be possible without Thanos knowing. So they'd lose their jobs anyway.'

'They're afraid to, you mean.'

Pethi looked straight and serious. 'If you had small children and thought it a real luxury to have meat to eat once a week, you might be a bit nervous.'

Tini said nothing, studying her fingers.

'You see, it's not simple. Ach,' he looked disgusted, 'you saw that fat . . . bah! In his rich Athenian suit. He who says he can't afford to finance more mining. Tonight he'll be eating roast sucking pig, while Spiros wonders how to pay for medicine for his little boy.'

'But . . . ' Tini said slowly. 'It doesn't make sense, does it? Suppose there *is* still some work in one of the mines. I mean, suppose the men are right, and it's not wishful thinking. Well, by doing nothing about it, Thanos will lose money himself in the end, won't he? The mines will just run down, and have to close. I should've thought it was worth him risking a bit of money, rather than that.'

'I tell you, he is an evil man. He will have a way of protecting himself, you can be sure.'

'To think he's a brother of Dimitrios. Aspassia was right – you would never believe it.'

'If Dimitrios still had some control in the mines, maybe then it would be better.'

'What do you mean?'

'Their father left them joint ownership of the land – he divided it equally, that is. And joint control of the mines there, with the approval of the Mining Company. Normally the elder son – Thanos – would have inherited the major share, and

48

had most control. But most people think he, their father, didn't trust Thanos to run the business honourably, and that Dimitrios would be the good influence.'

'So what happened?'

'Most of it happened before I was born, so I only know from the stories people tell, and what my mother's said. They always quarrelled, Thanos and Dimitrios. Dimitrios always wanted the men to be paid more, and refused a big salary himself. But Thanos wouldn't agree, and lived off the mines, refusing to spend money on new equipment or safety measures for the men. And as Thanos was in charge of the financial side of things, it was impossible for Dimitrios to get anywhere. In the end, he gave up. He let Thanos take over the whole thing. Dimitrios always wanted to be a fisherman, anyway, with his own fleet of boats, not a mine-owner. So he walked out. Thanos brought in a couple of assistants from Athens – people who'd agree with everything he said and did. But later, when I was a baby I think, Dimitrios wished he hadn't left, in some ways.'

'Why?'

'There was an accident, in one of the mines. People talked about it for years. Eleven men were killed and several were badly hurt. Dimitrios was mad with rage – he had warned Thanos about this mine, that if he didn't do certain things to increase safety, something could happen. Thanos had never taken any notice, and when the accident happened he denied that Dimitrios had ever said anything about it. Dimitrios blamed himself for leaving, for being weak with his brother. So he tried to make up for it – tried to get the families who'd lost their men to sue Thanos for neglecting the mine, but it was no use. Serifiots aren't sophisticated, and there was no money – but Thanos had riches to pay clever lawyers to disguise the truth, and nothing that Dimitrios said had any effect –'

'But – but that's not fair!'

Pethi almost laughed. 'Not fair! You believe the law should be fair. It runs on money.'

Tini was shocked. Pethi watched her pale face and felt sorry. He had the feeling that her whole idea of the island had taken a battering today. Now she had seen, under the sunlit exterior, the toughness and the poverty. He watched her glance towards the pathetic bunch of scraggy cats, and then to the arguing men. Pethi had spoken to fleeting tourists during summer months when he was helping his mother sell the rugs and lace she made: they saw only the romantic. Ah, how blue the sky, how white the houses. And the brilliance of the rugs. The delicious taverna dishes, ingeniously made from limited ingredients. The warmth of the people, weatherbeaten hospitable strength. But the tourists had left the island without seeing the suffering that could sometimes go with poverty, without glimpsing the corruption of men like Thanos. Now, Pethi thought, Tini would be thinking everything was bad, everything spoiled. But she would be wrong.

'So that's what Aspassia meant,' she said at last, 'when she said things happened here that made Zoë realize what Thanos was really like.'

'Yes.'

'Pethi, I just didn't know. That there could be so much unhappiness here. On this lovely island. I only saw ... I suppose I only saw what I liked. But I've heard all these sad stories. So sad ... '

For some reason, watching her sorrowful face, Pethi thought again of his secret cave.

'It's not all sad,' he said. 'I mean – we're not the only ones. Lots of people have a sad story. But it doesn't stop *life*. Does it?' He wondered if he had come anywhere near expressing what he meant.

She looked at him. 'That's true. If you mean, you get over things.' She paused, tinkling her spoon on her ice-cream dish. 'Like – like, for instance, when my mother died . . . do you know, I really hated Jason?'

Pethi didn't understand.

'She died when Jason was being born.'

'Oh. You thought it was his fault.'

'Yes. That's dreadful, isn't it?'

'I don't suppose so.'

'It's the first time I've actually said it. Actually told. Dad knew of course. He would.'

'Ha. Like you, you mean. Just "knowing" things.'

'A bit. But the thing was, he loved Jason, and I eventually realized it was pretty stupid to hate him. And Dad had loved my mother, I dare say even more than I had. She was . . . marvellous. Really, she was. But so is Jason, too, in a different kind of way.' Tini looked at Pethi, apologetic, a little embarrassed. 'I don't know why I said all that.'

The only sound was the men's argument, now reduced to an intense murmuring. Pethi stared at Tini in a strange surprise; it was as if he felt a kind of recognition.

'Tini,' he said. 'I want to tell you something. I want to tell you my secret. I really want to.'

5

They made the climbing walk slowly back to the upper village.

'Remember I said Vleppo has reason to hate Thanos?' Pethi bent to stroke the warm fur as the cat ran between them. 'That's really where it begins.'

Tini waited, wondering, as she watched the dust gathering on her toes from the dry road.

'Thanos likes shooting. Birds, that sort of thing. Well, a lot of people do. In some seasons we get a lot of small birds here that are good to eat. Anyway – the point about Thanos shooting is that he likes doing it just for the fun of killing things, not just for food. I mean, he'll kill swallows, just to amuse himself.'

'That's disgusting.'

He half-grinned at her reaction. 'You may find it's not all that uncommon. Or, at any rate, you won't find people are as shocked as you are. Not many Greeks are sentimental about animals.'

'Sentimental! There's a difference between that and not being cruel, isn't there?'

He shrugged. 'Yes, but . . . '

'Go on.'

'Well, Thanos is worse than most.' He scratched his head, considering how to tell the story. 'About four years ago, roughly, I was out on the clifftops' – he pointed – 'over that way. I was just walking, picking some herbs or something, and I heard shooting. Well, I wondered what was happening, so I kept going towards the shooting – it wasn't the season for any particular bird, as far as I remember. I came over the rocks near the old river bed, and saw Thanos. He was near the edge of the cliffs, and he was shooting at something on the ground, in a casual sort of way, and laughing. Well, it was peculiar, and I was curious, so I kept going.'

'Were you nervous?'

'No.' The suggestion surprised Pethi. 'I don't like Thanos, but he doesn't frighten me. Well – as I got nearer I could see that he was shooting at some kittens.'

'Kittens! *Kittens!*' Tini had stopped. 'What ever *for*?'

'I said. Amusement. They were crawling about on the clifftop, terrified by the noise, but not really seeming to know what was happening. There were six or seven of them. It was a litter one of his house cats had had, and he didn't want them, so thought he'd give himself a bit of sport getting rid of them. He brought them to the clifftop – maybe he was going to throw them over – and then decided shooting them would be more fun.'

Tini looked sick. 'Did he kill them?'

'When I got up to him they were all dead but two, and of course I distracted him, asking what he was doing. He was in a good mood, having a grand time, so he told me. Then he shot one of the last two, while I was standing there. He was delighted that I didn't like it.' Pethi kicked at the stones at the edge of the road. 'He was just going to shoot the last one, and I said – "No, leave that one. I'd like it" – I couldn't think how else to stop him. He laughed of course. It was a chance to upset me.

He couldn't stand me, because he knew I didn't like him, always pestering my mother, and at the same time he was saying publicly that he was going to marry a girl from a rich family in Athens – Damia, they called her – and as far as everyone knew the marriage arrangements were going ahead.'

'What's that got to do with the kittens?'

'Only that it gave me an idea at the time. Because when I said *I'd* have the kitten, Thanos just stood, laughing, ready to shoot, asking me if I was sure I wanted it. I was watching the kitten while Thanos was laughing at me. It was different from the others, bigger, and seemed to realize that Thanos was its enemy. It was spitting and snarling, and backing away. It backed away right to the edge of the cliff. I didn't know what to do. I could see it moving nearer and nearer to the edge, but was frightened that if I said anything, Thanos would just turn round and shoot it. I suppose I had some idea I could save it at the last minute.'

'What did you do?' Tini's eyes were enormous with suspense.

'I said – "Thanos, that kitten's going to be a fine cat" or something like that, and suggested that it would make a beautiful wedding present for Damia, his future bride.'

'Didn't that infuriate him?'

'He was quite taken aback for a second, and then he laughed again. I don't know if he thought I meant it or not, but it was just a desperate idea I had. I said it again – "think how unusual that would be, how anyone would be delighted with such a gift". When I think about it, it was ridiculous, when cats are everywhere on Serifos. But it was a particularly attractive kitten, so maybe I felt I could get away with it.'

'What did he do?'

'He said it was a wonderful idea, but that he would get more pleasure out of shooting it off the edge of the cliff. So he turned round, aiming his gun. Well, at that second, the kitten had backed right up to the edge, and before Thanos could shoot, it disappeared.

'It fell over!' Tini was near tears.

'I rushed up to the edge. Thanos was laughing himself sick of course. But the kitten was there, not far down, on a step, a small ledge. It was all right – only a metre or so down. Thanos realized by my face I suppose, and came to look. He aimed his gun again, but the kitten jumped down, to another ledge, and then another. Down this vast, sheer cliff. It's terribly high, with rocks at the bottom, and nobody had ever climbed there as far as I knew. Well, where the kitten was by now, it was almost impossible for Thanos to aim his gun properly. So he laughed at me again, and said – "all right, Pethi, if you want me to give that animal to Damia as a wedding present, you get it for me." He looked at me, very cunning. Of course, I knew what he meant.'

'What?'

'That it was a kind of bargain. If I got the kitten, he'd leave my mother alone. Only, of course, he thought I'd be killed in the attempt, so he couldn't lose.'

'It's true what you all say. He is evil.'

'So I said, yes, I'd get it. I don't think he expected that exactly, but he was practically helpless with laughter. "Go on, then," he kept saying, "go on then, down the cliff, down the cliff," and he was so certain that I would be dead before the day was finished, he walked away, back towards the village, in fact to hang around my mother again.'

'So you went after the kitten. Didn't you? Because it was Vleppo.'

Pethi sounded oddly weary, as if the very memory were tiring. 'That's right. I followed him down the cliff.'

'It must have been terrifying.'

'Yes. At first it was. But the strange thing was that the kitten wasn't at all afraid. It just kept going, almost leading me on. I went down the first few ledges, and it went down lower. It would stop, and wait, and as I got nearer, calling it, it would go on a bit more. After a while, although I was terrified at the drop, and wondering how I'd get back, I was interested too. There was something odd about it, the way this kitten was making its way down the cliff. It found a ledge, and followed it round. I discovered that the cliff itself was nothing like as sheer and smooth as it looked from the top, and although it was dangerous it wasn't by any means difficult to climb. So I tried not to think about it, and kept going, without looking down. Well, the cliff is part of a big cleft – another high cliff faces it. And the kitten led me round to a part where you can step from one cliff to the other, and then round another ledge on this other cliff.'

'It sounds awful.'

'No, it was much easier by then. But the point was, this ledge leads to a cave. It's a cave in the middle of this sheer cliff, one that has legends and superstitions attached – I've heard fishermen say it's haunted – and it's supposed to be absolutely inaccessible.'

'But you – and Vleppo – got there.'

'That's right. We did. He followed the ledge, and stopped, and just jumped inside. And I went in after him.'

56

Pethi said no more. They arrived at the stony junction of the mule track and the road, and turned to trudge up the short cut. Tini waited a few minutes. And then: 'So that's it. That's where your secret is.'

'Yes, but – ' Pethi stopped, looked at Tini. 'I don't want to tell any more. I'd like to show you. Show you the cave, and the secret.'

'You mean – I'd have to climb down that cliff, like you did?'

'I know the way now. By heart. I can do it without thinking, even. I'm sure I could take you. Really, it would be safe.' He felt sure it was possible. For at the same time he knew it was important, and perhaps inevitable too.

Tini looked at his sober, black eyes. 'All right,' she said, almost whispered. He convinced her, though she didn't know why.

'We'll go this afternoon.' It was as if he couldn't wait, now the story was told.

'Pethi – your boat. Didn't you want to sail her today?'

'Yes,' he agreed, 'But she'll wait.' As if the cave wouldn't.

Inexplicably, Tini stopped being afraid. Such confidence was perhaps infectious. She remembered that the story hadn't ended yet.

'What happened? When you took the kitten back?'

'I met Thanos leaving our house. He was in a filthy mood. My mother had more or less thrown him out, with the help of a few acid words from Aspassia. I think he'd told her that if I was out of the way she'd come round to thinking she could do with a rich husband, and it was only shame at having a son and no husband that made her refuse him. I gather my mother went into a rage at this – she has quite a temper – ' Pethi

57

smiled at his own understatement, ' – and up to then she'd managed to hold Thanos off by being cool and unco-operative. Only this time he made her furious.'

'Surely he didn't think she'd change her mind and marry him at that kind of approach?'

'Only the gods know what Thanos thought or ever thinks. He wanted power over her like he wants over everything, and he wanted to punish her too for not being impressed by him.'

'Oh.'

'Well, there he was, leaving the house. So I held out the kitten, and said, "It's yours, Thanos, for your bride Damia." I knew I would infuriate him, but I suppose I was angry too at seeing him at the house again. He went absolutely white, and then he walked up to me fast, and knocked the kitten out of my hands, on to the ground, and then walked away. The kitten – Vleppo – crouched and spat at him.'

'And he's done that ever since.'

'Yes.' He paused. They had nearly reached their houses. 'So. I asked my mother if I might keep him. Vleppo. She said yes, if I was totally responsible for his food. It seemed important to keep him. Because of the cave . . . and – oh, well, it's hard to explain.'

'You called him Vleppo, "I see", because of the cave, too.'

'Yes.'

Tini sat for a while on a rock. 'And what about Damia, the girl from Athens?'

Pethi's mouth turned down in contempt. 'She was a fool. She came to his house, and she's there today, still. Living there. Of course he didn't marry her. He took the money she brought with her, but she still waits for the wedding.'

'Poor thing. She must have loved him.'

'Perhaps. If so she is the only person who does. But what can she do but stay? Unless she were to go away and be alone. She can't go back to her family – she's dishonoured.'

'Dishonoured?'

'Certainly. And in some places, if she had brothers, they would have come to revenge their family.'

Tini stared. 'These days?'

Pethi nodded. 'In some parts.'

'And she had no brothers?'

'No. And her father died. So Thanos wins.'

'Poor thing,' said Tini again, somehow reminded of the pathetic island cats and their haunted faces, trapped by circumstances. The many things she had learned about Serifos that morning reeled confusedly in her brain.

'I dare say she's all right,' Pethi said. 'At any rate she's clothed and housed, and I expect she does care for Thanos a little. It could be worse.'

Tini leapt up. 'I said I'd get lunch ready. Dad's painting the house. When will we go to the cave?'

'When you're ready. I've got to whitewash Aphrodite's shed, but after that – '

'Whose?'

'Aphrodite's.' Pethi laughed at her face. 'The goat. I started the whitewashing yesterday.'

'I'll come and help. Could I?'

He nodded. 'All right. Then we'll go.' She started up the hill towards the pink house, and he called after her. 'Wear shoes you can climb in, remember.'

*　　*　　*

'Now,' gasped Tini, 'I know what you meant when you said Vleppo was a good rock-climber.' She flopped shaking into the cave mouth. 'I could have done with some extra toes myself.'

Pethi pulled himself into the cave, and sat with his legs dangling out. He looked at Tini and felt happier than he had felt with any previous friends. And, barely admitting it, he sneakingly knew that Nikos and Stavros and the others wouldn't have climbed these cliffs so readily. 'You did all right,' was all he said.

She rolled on to her front, and hung her head out of the cave, staring down the dizzy cliff to the sea, then across the cleft to the cliff they had left behind. 'Did we really come all that way?' She began to feel triumphant. 'Imagine.' Then giggled, tremblingly. 'Good thing you told me not to look down.'

Pethi fidgeted. 'Are you ready? To go on, I mean?' Vleppo waited, bright eyes on them both.

She sat up. 'Yes. Is it difficult?'

'No, but it's dark. Hang on to my shirt. I've got my torch, and Vleppo can find his way anyhow. We go down quite steeply, but it's not dangerous.'

'Then what?'

'You'll see.'

They plunged into the black depths of the cliff. Tini scrambled blindly after Pethi, excited, wondering. Once she caught hold of his arm as she slipped, and she could feel his tension. Showing her the cave, telling her his secret, she knew it was momentous.

When they arrived at the first great cavern, and Pethi's torch beam lit up the astounding beauty of the stalactites, Tini was dumb, awestruck. The colours were jewels as the light swung upon them.

'Well?' Pethi was disappointed at her silence.

'Pethi. It's . . . amazing. Beautiful.' But she was distractedly aware of a buzzing, singing sensation in her temples that she had never known. 'Beautiful,' she murmured again.

'This way.'

The feeling increased as they moved behind the end of the stalactites and into the circular, inner cave. As Tini stared round at the glistening rocks, veined with red and blue, she was aware that her skin had become icy cool, with a chill that was separate from that of the sunless underground air. Was her hair rising from her head? That was how it felt. And in her brain, humming. Like distant voices, or music. It was strange. What was it? She didn't feel ill. Far from it. She felt relaxed and well. It was . . . yes, it was a pleasurable feeling, and mysterious. She stood, considering it. Perhaps it would pass. But no, it remained. And as Pethi led her slowly into the cave, it even grew.

'Pethi,' she said softly. 'Pethi, I feel funny.'

He stopped. 'Do you?' He stared in the twilight into Tini's absorbed face. Did it, then, happen to anyone who came here – this feeling of strength and power that he knew again, spreading through his being? He hesitated, far from sure that he could share that much of his secret.

'Funny in what way?'

'Like . . . dizzy. No, not exactly. I can't explain.'

He was oddly relieved. 'Reaction to the climbing, that's all,' he said briskly. 'Here, sit down.' He drew her across the cave to the lighter part. She sat on the rock floor, cool and smooth.

61

Pethi watched her. 'All right?'

'Fine. Really, I'm fine.' She was sure the feeling would go soon. 'You're right I expect – just reaction. I don't feel ill. Anyway, I'm not the fainting kind.'

'Ready, then? For the real secret?'

Tini nodded, suddenly apprehensive.

Pethi's hands were light and strong on her shoulders. He turned her round slightly. 'Look. Just there, on the floor.'

As she turned, she saw in the diffused light a short distance away from her on the cave floor, the face of a woman. And gasped. It was sculpted in pure, white marble; a calm, lovely face, seeming to look directly at Tini. The eyes were large, and wide. The lips curving, the jaw strong. It was a decisive face, and yet delicately female. Above a clear forehead her hair waved back a short way, to disappear under the rim of what appeared to be a helmet. The sculpted neck was smooth, exquisite, strong. And there it ended, at the throat, broken off. Leaning forward to look behind it, Tini saw that the back of the helmet too was broken, so that the head leaned back at an angle on the floor in the same way that a head rests upon a pillow. But the face was perfect, without crack or blemish.

Tini realized she had been gazing, silent, for some moments. Pethi waited. 'Who is this?' she finally asked, dreamily, although in the back of her humming brain she sensed she already knew the answer.

Pethi kneeled beside her. 'I believe,' he said softly, 'she is the goddess Athene. See – the helmet, for the goddess of war who liked to make peace between people. I've seen pictures of statues of her, and she looks like this sometimes.' Tini, looking up at Pethi's face, saw a strength she had not noticed before in his expression, and heard it in his voice even though he spoke quietly.

'Yes. I've seen the one that was on the pediment of the Parthenon in Athens. It is a bit like this. Pethi – do you mean, this is ancient too? Classical?' She tried to recall the conversation Pethi had had with her father, but it was an irretrievable distance away. What was the matter with her?

'I don't know anything about it really. Only . . . only I *feel* . . . yes, that it is ancient.'

'It's marble.' Tini leaned forward to gaze into the calm face.

'I think it might be marble from Paros, because it's so white. I cleaned it up a bit, it was dirty. The marble on Serifos isn't as pure as that.'

'There must be more of her', Tini realized. 'And why is she here?'

Pethi shrugged. 'Perhaps people hid her. They used to hide treasures in ancient times if there were enemies invading, like the Turks. Maybe it got broken, or maybe this was all they could rescue.'

'Oh, Pethi. I don't blame you at all, not wanting people to know. This cave . . . everything.' Her ideas about archaeology and discoveries and encouraging prosperity in the island seemed to have vanished. 'It's so . . . mysterious, the whole place. And she – she's beautiful. Incredibly beautiful.'

Tini reached out her hands slowly, in some awe, to touch the smooth marble features. Watching her, Pethi observed with a small corner of his mind that Tini's fingers themselves had a marble-pale texture.

And then something terrifying happened.

As Tini's hand touched the glistening sculpture, she

63

suddenly threw her head back, her eyes staring upwards, as if she had been struck, and uttered a strange and chilling cry.

Pethi was on his feet. 'What is it? What's wrong?'

She said nothing.

'Are you hurt?' He stared aghast at her blank face.

She ignored him. Instead, to Pethi's horror, she began to talk, very fast, in a language he didn't recognize.

'Tini!' cried Pethi. His heart was banging strangely. 'What are you saying? Stop that. Stop it, Tini.'

But she didn't stop. Her brilliant blue eyes seemed not to see him. Her pale hair streamed back from her forehead, shining faintly in the cave's dim light. And she talked. A string of extraordinary words, running rapidly together in a high monotone. It was as if she had gone mad.

Pethi grew angry. Surely it was a trick she was playing. He shouted at her: 'If this is a British joke I think it is completely stupid, *stupid*.' And then, 'You've ruined my secret, and I'm going.' Turning, he started to march back across the cave. But he found it wasn't that easy. The mysterious strength that he usually felt in this place seemed now to be pulling him back; as if his will to leave was being defeated by it. Or was it just that Tini's voice, despite his furious words, hadn't wavered?

He stopped, and looked back. She sat in the glow of light, her lovely fair profile clear against the rocks. Her strange words still poured out, and now, gradually, her voice was growing lower, calmer. Pethi's anger vanished; he knew this was no trick. It was something outside Tini's control. She wasn't aware of him.

64

It was then that Pethi noticed Vleppo.

In the excitement of bringing Tini here, he had forgotten the cat. But there he was, sitting beside Tini herself. Not merely sitting, but sitting close to her, watching her, his yellow eyes round with intense interest. Pethi had never seen him so near to anyone but himself. Later, it occurred to him that he had not even felt remotely jealous. Instead, his main sensation was of realizing, in surprise, that Vleppo understood something that he himself did not. Somewhere, in the back of his brain, there was something he should be understanding . . . something just out of reach . . . what was it? He walked slowly back across the cave towards Tini and his cat.

Tini's voice came gently now. The words were beautiful, rhythmic. They flowed, they rolled, murmuring round the crystalline rocks. Pethi was calm now, unafraid, kneeling near her, and aware of an infinite sense of peace and wellbeing spreading around and through him. Again, that feeling that he could do anything in the world. And at the same time, with a thrill of disbelief, Pethi realized what was this strange language that Tini spoke. And, almost as quickly, he knew how to make her stop.

'Tini,' he said gently, and took hold of her hands, lifting them with strength and confidence from the cool marble face. 'Tini.'

She looked straight at him, seeing again.

'Pethi.' She frowned. 'I'm freezing. Oh no – don't tell me I fainted.'

'I suppose you did, in a way.'

'Oh – and I've not even looked at your goddess properly.' But Pethi held on firmly to her hands, pulling her to her feet.

As he did, he heard the owl's shrill shriek somewhere high in the roof of the cave.

'No. Leave her. We must go. Now. Come on.'

'But . . . Pethi.' She dragged her feet. 'What – ?'

'Wait. Let's get out to the sun. I'll tell you.'

He pulled her, fingers firm round her wrist, through to the stalactite cavern. Tini, feeling curiously tired, leant on his strength and followed. Vleppo came close behind.

At the cave mouth the sun was a golden, comforting greeting. Pethi insisted they sat there for a while. 'The climb back isn't easy, and you look pale.' He himself felt drained of energy now that the goddess' cave was behind them. He sat quietly, looking out at the calm blue of sky and sea, vaguely aware of a tremor of reaction in his fingers. What had happened? He was no longer strong, with an instinctive understanding. He was confused, even nervous. And guilty too. He glanced at Tini. She looked tired. Probably he should never have brought her here. What were they involved in now?

Tini smiled at him, hesitating to ask why he looked troubled. Something strange had happened, but what?

'Don't worry,' she said. 'I feel fine.'

He looked out at the sky again, serious, silent. He would tell her, she felt, whatever it was, once away from here.

'Let's go,' he suggested.

They climbed slowly and carefully. At the opposite clifftop, they flopped among wild flowers, saying nothing. Vleppo settled weightily in the small of Pethi's back as he lay spread out, getting his breath. Then, Tini said:

66

'I know it was something peculiar. Wasn't it?'

Something so inexplicable was almost impossible to describe to her. But gradually Pethi told her about the atmosphere and happenings in the cave: their skins crept coldly, although the sun shone.

Tini's eyes were enormous. 'I can't believe it.' She was frightened. 'You mean, as soon as I touched her, it started? This talking?'

'Immediately.'

'But I don't remember it. Anything. Except I felt funny – I said so – when we went into the cave. A kind of humming in my head, distant humming. It's . . . horrible.'

'No. It wasn't horrible. It was frightening at first. And I was angry too, thinking you were playing some joke on me. But then it was peaceful. I can't explain exactly. It's more frightening now, away from the cave, thinking and talking about it afterwards. But it wasn't then.'

'But what was I saying?'

Pethi scratched at some leaves under his fingers.

'I don't know. Only – '

'What? *What*?'

'It was too fast at first. I couldn't understand. It just sounded like – nonsense. I thought you might have gone mad, even. But then, near the end, you were speaking much more slowly and I thought . . . I *think* . . . ' he took a breath, 'that it was all ancient Greek.' He watched her face.

Her mouth opened, and shut.

'It can't have been,' she managed eventually, very low. 'That's ridiculous. I don't know any ancient Greek. Dad does,

67

but I've never learned any. Not a word. I only ever learned modern Greek. That's all.'

Neither said anything for a few minutes.

Then Pethi said, almost apologetically, 'I don't see what else it could have been.'

'Couldn't it have been modern Greek, only very fast and mixed up?'

He shook his head. 'Don't you see, I do know some ancient Greek. I learned it at school. Some words are similar, some the same exactly as the modern ones, but only a few. And you said a few words I recognized – like 'sákos', which usually means shield, and 'drákontes' which I think must be snakes.'

'Snakes!' Tini stared at him.

'Can't you remember anything?' he pleaded.

'I can't. You know how it is, when you wake up just after a dream, and the dream's disappeared – you know it was there, but you can't catch it, can't remember it. I feel a bit like that. A bit. As if I know something was happening, but I don't know what.'

They looked at each other.

'Pethi. It's frightening. I'm frightened, I really am.' She twisted her cold hands.

He almost grinned. 'It isn't a very reasonable thing to happen, is it?'

She remembered something. 'Pethi! Is that what you meant this morning, when you asked me – about whether some things aren't reasonable, are mysterious?' She looked as if she might be angry. 'Did you know this would happen?'

'Don't be stupid.' He dismissed it with finality.

She was relieved. 'What, then?'

He slanted a look at her. 'It's hard to explain. It's the cave. The feeling it's always given *me*. I didn't expect it, or anything like it, to happen to anyone else.'

'What feeling?'

'It sounds ridiculous as soon as it's described. But in there, I'm strong. Not just strong, but powerful – as if anything's possible.' He stopped, sure he had come nowhere near an adequate description.

But she remembered. 'Yes, Yes. I think I sensed it, once or twice. I do remember that.' She understood.

'And something else.' Pethi paused, thinking. 'Vleppo.' The cat shifted on Pethi's back, a warm soft weight. 'He was strange, too. He sat right next to you, staring at you, as if he could understand what you were saying. Really. It surprised me. Not just because he was taking notice of you and not of me, but because there was something he seemed to know and accept – and I'd always thought animals reacted against anything a bit supernatural.'

'Supernatural.' Tini scraped her hair back from her face, nervously. 'I don't like it. Things you don't understand.'

Pethi said slowly, 'But they happen. Greeks know it. It's part of our tradition.' Something seemed to dawn on him, and he sat up, facing Tini, tipping Vleppo off his back with the movement. The cat glared, indignantly washing himself as if soiled by such lack of consideration.

'In the cave, Tini,' Pethi said, 'I had this sensation that there was something I should be understanding, but I couldn't grasp it. Maybe I never will. But whatever it was, whatever happened, there's something I seem to know, instinctively. And that is, that whatever it was you said, in

69

what I believe was ancient Greek, was something to do with her – it was *all* to do with her – with the goddess Athene.'

The air whispered along the clifftops.

'Oh. Oh, Pethi.'

'What's the matter?'

'My name.'

'Tini.'

'Yes. But you see. It's really Athene.'

Pethi saw only her pale face and huge eyes. 'What?' he whispered.

'I've always been called Tini. I just forget most of the time, but my real name's Athene.'

They gazed at one another, suspended.

'Athene . . . '

Every tiny sound around them disappeared. The wind dropped and died. The sea stopped rushing at the rocks. They sat motionless in the lowering sunlight and bright flowers, not even hearing a heartbeat. The clear, rosy air seemed charged with fearful wonder, with some extraordinary secrets that they might never properly see.

Then Vleppo yawned rudely with a slight yowl, bringing them back with a reminder that he was hungry. The wind tossed at their hair again, the sea moved, and a donkey brayed honkingly across the valley.

Pethi got up, his cat at once winding round his legs.

'Tini,' he said, 'you understand, don't you, why I didn't want anyone – your father, archaeologists – to know about her? About the cave, and everything?' He took her hand and pulled her up.

They stood still, looking across the soaring cliffs to the dark cave mouth, now remote but still mysterious.

'Of course I do. How couldn't I?'

Tini didn't take her hand from Pethi's, and he felt disinclined to drop it. They walked back to the village saying very little.

6

The village was shouting and scurrying, filled with *fasaría*, a fuss and noise. Pethi and Tini were jolted back into the everyday life of the island by running feet, high-pitched arguments in doorways, glasses jumping as men banged taverna tables, and once, the sound of weeping from an open shutter. The narrow streets echoed, the first lights of the evening flickered. What had happened here?

'Eh, Pethi!' someone called from a window, seeing them, 'it's a bad night, a bad night for Serifos, is it not?' But disappeared, assuming Pethi knew all, to shout at someone within.

'What's going on? Everyone's so angry.' Tini felt irritated, snatched from their pensive walk back from the cave.

Pethi began to hurry. 'Something. I don't know about angry, but everyone's talking about it. The mines. Something to do with the mines, it must be.'

'Talking!' Tini mocked. 'Greeks always sound as if they're quarrelling, even if they're discussing what time they'll eat dinner.' Pethi ignored this, clutching at the arm of a man disappearing into one of the houses: Tini knew his face – he had been at Tassos' cafe this morning, shouting at Thanos.

'Spiros – what's going on? Not an accident?'

Spiros stopped on one foot, making rapid polite greetings to boy and girl. 'Ach, this is no accident,' he raged, foam at the

72

corners of his mouth, 'it is a plan. A wicked plan of that evil Thanos.' Spiros was shaking with inarticulate anger. 'Everybody is fired from his mines!' he burst out. And went.

'Everybody!' The shock.

They ran the rest of the way without knowing why.

By the olive tree beside Zoë's house, a small group of people stood. Zoë herself, pale and bitter, her arms around a wailing Aspassia. Across Aspassia's head, she and Dimitrios exchanged rapid, flat, angry comments. Dimitrios looked awful, white-lipped, older. Three or four neighbours stood with them, a woman weeping quietly, some men arguing pointlessly.

Dimitrios told them what had happened. Thanos had sacked every man, that afternoon, from his remaining workable mines, saying it was a decision from the Mining Company in Athens. He had said how sorry he was, how he would suffer a great personal loss – Dimitrios could not express enough contempt at this – but nothing could be done.

Exactly how many men were out of work wasn't clear, but it was too many. They knew it would be a waste of time to apply to other mines on the island for work: they would need no extra labour. A group of them had come to Dimitrios, demanding that he find out why Thanos had done this to them, to their families, to the island. Some of them, in their fear and desperation, had turned on their friend Dimitrios, saying he had failed them by leaving the mines all those years ago. Dimitrios himself felt that this was true, and had no adequate answer. But had promised he would find out what he could, and help if possible.

But he felt it was hopeless. He had gone to Thanos' house, but he wasn't there. They said he was in Athens. Dimitrios was angry, angrier than Pethi had ever seen him; and it was a frightening anger, because it was cold and controlled.

'All the men will go,' wept Aspassia. 'It is the end of Serifos. The gods have put a curse on this island.' She wailed within Zoë's comforting arms. Tini's eyes met Pethi's. He drew her away from the group.

'You go on home. I don't suppose you're in the mood for all this fuss. I've got to milk Aphrodite. Say to George to come down with you a bit later, and eat with us this evening. And Jason. And we can talk about it a bit more calmly.'

'Will that be all right with Zoë?'

Pethi nodded briefly. 'I'll tell her.' He paused. 'I want to think about it. Everything that's happened.'

Tini hovered. Something in his seriousness worried her. He was tense, suddenly unhappy. She didn't like going now.

'Go on.' He turned away towards Aphrodite's shed. 'See you later.' She watched him go round the side of the little white house before she walked slowly up the hill.

Aphrodite's amber eyes were fiendish as she stamped near the bucket, sensing the unease that hummed around the village. Pethi leaned his head on her warm side and sang her a calm song while his thoughts untangled.

With unwelcome clarity, he saw he had a choice to make. The work had been taken from the men of his village and the village of the harbour. They would leave. The island would die. He didn't see how Thanos could be forced to give them back their jobs. Surely he couldn't have risked firing all the men without the total agreement of the Mining Company.

Other work was needed for Serifos. Pethi knew that providing it rested with him.

By the time the goat had given all the milk she intended, the house was quieter. The neighbours had gone back to their own homes, Aspassia and Dimitrios had gone indoors with Zoë. They sat, talking quietly now.

But in Pethi's mind there was no peace. Unravelling his thoughts one way had ended only in another kind of confusion. Too much had happened today at the cave. Too much had happened here, in the village. He was pulled in different directions. As he carried the fresh, warm milk into the house he had no idea what he would do.

When he had strained the milk into clean cans, he took the chance to thank Dimitrios for his work on the *Petros*. It was good to think of his beautiful boat again, one clear, fine thing in the middle of it all. 'Ah, Pethi,' the fisherman's face brightened a little, his arm hugging Pethi's shoulders tightly, 'it is as I promised, and no more. For you, I am happy that it is a good day.'

* * *

Under the lamp outside the door, the cool air was mellow-lit. Zoë and George sipped small glasses of *ouzo*, a powerful aniseed-tasting drink which neither parent would allow their children to try. 'Yet', they qualified.

Instead, Pethi and Tini drank a clear golden wine, made on the island. They sat quietly, sometimes glancing at each other, letting the adults talk. Vleppo curled near Pethi's feet; Jason sat by him, a toy in his hands, concentrating on his own world. In a few minutes, Dimitrios and Aspassia returned to join them, pouring out more *ouzo*. Aspassia added a plate of fat black olives to the dishes on the table. Chunks of white goat's cheese, slices of salt fish.

George pounced greedily on the olives.

'Intelligent habits, the Greeks have,' he said comfortably. 'All these good things to eat with drinks before dinner. And look at Jason there. Imagine him up and about at this hour in London. The neighbours would report me for neglect. But here, we snooze in the hot afternoon, and live at night.' He put a large lump of goat cheese in his mouth.

'You like the cheese?' Zoë asked hospitably.

'Irreproachable.'

'Pethi made it.'

Pethi came out of a deep thought. 'With the goat's help,' he said modestly.

'You can make cheese?' Tini was impressed, expressing appreciation by eating more. Pethi smiled at her because her face was so exquisite in the lamplight. She smiled back, but faintly, feeling vaguely jittery, wondering what Pethi had worked out in his thoughts, what he would say.

When they went indoors to eat the dish of fish baked with tomatoes and garlic that Zoë had prepared, talk of the mines came up again. While the adults argued and theorized, Tini valiantly tried not to eat too much of the delicious food, weighted by her knowledge of island poverty. She had learned that Zoë and Pethi lived frugally, their income earned only from rugs and lace that Zoë could sell in the summer, from selling goat's milk and cheese, and from odd jobs that Pethi could do. Their small walled garden was stocked with vegetables and vines, and they kept some hens. Compared with many Serifiots, they were well off. But Tini was comparing with her life in London, with good meat every day. Still, despite her efforts, Zoë heaped more food on Tini's plate, her dark eyes shining at the girl's compliments.

'You said Thanos was up to something,' Pethi was saying to Dimitrios. 'What, for instance?'

Dimitrios pulled down his mouth. 'Something. I don't know what. But something.' It didn't help much.

'He ought to lose money by sacking everyone,' Zoë said. 'It doesn't make sense.'

'But if the Mining Company doesn't believe there's any more work –'

Pethi was interrupted by Dimitrios: 'Bah!' he cried. 'That brother of mine would convince them, if it were in his own interest.'

'Then,' Pethi tried, 'can't we find out what he's said to them? Find out the truth?'

'We can try,' Dimitrios said, but without hope. Evidently he felt that the authorities were far too powerful for mere honesty to succeed.

Pethi pulled a piece of bread into shreds. If only there were some way of getting the men their jobs back. If it were true that Thanos was up to something – if this wasn't just dark suspicion on Dimitrios' part, born of anger and frustration – and they could expose his plan, then perhaps, perhaps . . .

'I suppose the men will leave,' George said.

Zoë's oval face was sad in the oil lamp's gleam. 'They'll leave,' she nodded. 'Already they're talking of Australia and Germany.'

Pethi didn't look at Tini. 'George,' he said. And stopped.

'Yes?'

77

'When you – when you begin your explorations, your archaeological ones, wanting to dig things up here – won't you need men to work for you. To dig? I mean, apart from experts?'

Tini didn't breathe.

George agreed. 'Indeed yes. If it should come to anything, quite a lot of workers would be needed.'

'Well.' Pethi crumbled more bread. 'Miners dig, don't they?'

'You're saying, we could give the miners a good job. Yes.' George nodded again. 'They'd be ideal, extremely useful. But – '

'But what?' Zoë said, diving into the kitchen.

'But they need jobs *now*. Not in several months' time. Don't they?'

Everyone agreed.

'It would probably be months,' George went on, 'even if I started tomorrow, working things out, before I'd even know if there was to be any excavation at all. And then there'd be more time to wait while I got permission for a dig, and money to be found to finance it. It could be a year, years even, before the actual work began, And there's no guarantee that I'll ever find anything anyway.'

There was silence in the little room. Tini watched Pethi's face in a confused panic. He opened his mouth to speak, and closed it again. He looked at Tini, and stayed silent.

Zoë, coming back into the room with coffee, saw their faces. And wondered. 'What are you two – ?' she began, but gave up when they looked at her blankly.

Pethi took down a dictionary from the small shelf in his room before he got into bed. Modern and ancient Greek. He flicked over the dusty pages. They were there, the words he had recognized. 'Drákontes'. 'Sákos'. Snakes. Shield.

In bed, he lay back, achingly tired. Vleppo's warm weight settled over his feet. Shield, snakes. Unexpectedly, it came into his head: the myth. Athene. She was the goddess who carried a shield. He remembered it from books. And on it, now he could picture it, was fixed the head of Medusa, the fearsome head which instead of hair wore a mass of writhing snakes. It was the sight of this grotesque face, snake-surrounded, which, said the legend, turned Athene's enemies to stone.

Pethi fell asleep, his own confused thoughts writhing and intertwined.

*　　*　　*

He woke up and stared straight at the moon.

Tini's voice had broken into his sleep. He sat up. Tini's voice? But she wasn't there. A dream, then. What had she said? Pethi caught echoes of Tini's voice still, urging him.

'To the boats, go down to the boats,' he heard it lingering in his mind. That was what she had said.

Then Pethi froze, utterly awake. The voice he was remembering was Tini's voice from the cave of the goddess, not her own. It had spoken in ancient Greek and he had understood it. In his dream. Telling him in ancient Greek to go down to the boats. In the middle of the night.

His bare feet touched the floor, his clothes were pulled on. 'Vleppo,' he whispered, looking towards the end of the bed. And then realized with a slight shiver that Vleppo was sitting by the door, waiting for him. Ready.

The island was still and silver. Pethi felt compelled to creep, to slink among the glittering rocks, plunging from shadow to shadow. He had never feared the night, but now something unknown quivered in the air, something to make him quiet and furtive. In the village the houses were whitely poised, steps gleaming, black shadows clear cut on the walls. Vleppo walked close to Pethi's feet; the warmth of him brushed reassuringly against cold ankles from time to time. 'To the boats, go down to the boats . . . ' He walked on as if pulled on a thread.

Down the road, after the mule track, Pethi hugged the rocky side. The glimmering ribbon of road should have been an attraction; a place to walk boldly in the moonlight, with one's shadow, owning the night. But he stayed at the side, walking fast. The whole world shimmered.

Beside the harbour he waited in the shadow of a narrow street, looking out at the spangled water between the tamarisk trees, where a few masts swayed. To the boats? Which boats? Not thinking, following instinct, he turned in the direction of Dimitrios' boats, and his own. Swiftly he moved from dark doorway to doorway along the harbour, along the cafés and tavernas, alleyway openings and house porches that were the backdrop to the quay. When he was opposite the wooden jetty, he stopped, waiting.

There was almost total silence: just the faint noise of licking water, that was all.

Nothing was happening at the jetty. What had he expected? Hardly any boats were there, for Dimitrios' fleet was out fishing along with most of the other men's boats. Pethi crept out into the brilliant moonlight, forward to where the *Petros* lay glossily on the water. There was no movement, no life, nothing.

Pethi stood near the boat's shadow and looked along the harbour's curve. The moon picked out every shape in silver; he could have read a book by its clear light. Nobody could be seen. No shadow crossed the quay. No window blinked light. No sound. It was as if the island had been deserted, as if everyone had sailed secretly away.

'To the boats?' It began to creep into Pethi's mind that he had been a fool, and that tomorrow morning he would feel even more stupid. To follow a voice in a dream. A dream, that was all, after a day of tension and confusion. To come down here, following a voice he imagined, at dead of night, to find . . . nothing. Nothing.

In a second he was furious with himself, hissing at Vleppo: 'Come on. Back home.' And strode along the jetty away from his boat. How stupid to have come. He must have been half asleep.

But when he turned at the end of the jetty to call Vleppo again, he was surprised. The cat hadn't followed him. He sat, gleaming silver-black in the moon: his eyes glowed wide and calm. 'Vleppo?' Pethi stopped. The cat waited, not moving.

Pethi stood wondering. And as he hesitated, over the harbour rooftops came a sound: the high squeaky mewing call of a little owl.

In that second, without him even being aware of either fear or excitement, Pethi felt his heart begin to beat rapidly. He stared at Vleppo, expecting some kind of signal now. Vleppo stood, blinked his eyes, and jumped smoothly aboard the *Petros*. Without thinking, and with a sensation of having no real choice, Pethi followed.

81

Well outside the harbour mouth, but clearly through the still night, came the noise of a boat's engine. It was a fast engine, not a fishing boat.

Pethi sat in the shadows by the wheel. Vleppo sat beside him, one large warm paw resting on his knee. The engine noise was louder; now, surely, the boat was in the harbour.

Pethi stood, slowly, peering out. Clearly it came, a white launch cutting aggressively through the quiet water, tossing brilliant foam. The engine was fairly loud, but no louder than many of the boats that would come and go through the night: nobody in the village was likely to awake hearing anything unexpected. But now the engine cut down, the boat slowed. And Pethi saw that it was undoubtedly making for his jetty, away from the main pier where the steamers called, away from the main concentration of houses. He ducked back into the deep shadows again. As his hand rested on Vleppo's back, he felt the inner rumble of a cat's growl, a deep swearing tremble, not yet a real sound, but hostile. And he knew who would be on the launch. He kept his head down.

It was near. The water moved and rocked the *Petros*. Now the launch engine cut out completely to allow the craft to drift in to the jetty. As its sound disappeared, men's voices rang clearly. 'So this is Serifos,' Pethi heard. A deep voice with a strange foreign accent. And then some words he couldn't hear, several voices.

At that moment Pethi's insides turned horribly. The white launch came sliding in, right alongside the *Petros*. He shrank. Why it was so essential to keep hidden, he hardly knew, but he hardly knew the reasons for anything after the past day.

Thanos was the first to jump on the jetty. He seemed to

tower darkly, taller in the night. Pethi could see the amber *kombolói* swinging between his fingers, the beads gleaming in the moon's light. Vleppo quivered with inward growls.

A second man stepped on to the jetty heavily: he said something to Thanos, continuing some previous conversation. No words were clear. Thanos laughed cheerfully. 'Good god, Marko,' he said, the words quite loud, 'the price is better than that where we'll be selling, don't worry. And silver like this – well . . . ' he laughed again, slapping the man Marko on the shoulder. Marko answered in a murmur and chuckled too.

Three more men stepped on to the jetty, talking quietly to each other. Pethi craned to see them without being seen, and without revealing himself to a man left on board the white launch, at the wheel.

One of the men was very short, stocky. He was speaking to Thanos. Pethi heard again the foreign accent that he had no way of placing. 'An isle of riches, eh?' he said, perhaps cynically, looking along the quiet, innocent harbour. Thanos swung his beads and answered quietly but clearly. 'For us, my friend, for us,' then turned to dismiss the man in the launch with a few quick, sharp words, telling him to return to Piraeus as arranged.

If the men continued to speak then, their voices were covered by the roar of the launch's engine as the boat left the jetty, turning in a spray of silver to cut across the harbour and away at speed. Thanos and his four companions were off the jetty and on the quayside before the sound had died away, and walking quickly towards the shadows.

Pethi and Vleppo slunk off the *Petros*. It was, Pethi felt, urgent to follow them and try to hear what was said. Something was happening, important to Serifos. Thanos had brought these

83

strangers here at night, men who had never seen the island before, and they talked of riches. Riches on Serifos? Again Pethi heard the voice of the goddess in his dream, urging him to the boats. He must listen, and know what Thanos was going to do.

Hugging the jetty rail, he reached the quay. The men were moving along at the back: Pethi saw them cross a moonlit gap between the houses. If he moved fast he could get through the bright patch between the jetty and the shadows without them seeing him; they were, after all, facing away from him. He streaked over the stones, Vleppo with him, soundlessly.

The men didn't hesitate. They were talking among themselves, and their leather-soled town shoes scuffed on the pavings: a boy's bare feet and a cat's paws were unlikely to catch their attention.

Gradually, slinkingly, Pethi and Vleppo caught up on the group. Nearer, nearer. Until they were only four or five metres behind. Pethi dared get no closer than that.

Frustratingly, only half-sentences reached him, and none seemed to make sense. Thanos' was the clearest voice. 'To-morrow' he said, 'we take a look at the site, all right?' Pethi couldn't hear the reply from the man Marko. Thanos went on: 'Otherwise, stick to the house, keep out of the way.' Two of the men murmured something, then one said 'miners', and Pethi caught the word 'Dimitrios'. Thanos laughed slightly, and his reply was lower. Still, Pethi heard him say 'Mining Company', and a little later, 'that brother, he can be dealt with'. Another laugh.

Pethi tried to creep closer, but at that point the men reached the bright beginning of a street, and Thanos turned abruptly, leading the men into it. It was one of the streets leading to a small square. Pethi stopped, Vleppo at his heels.

He could hear the men walking on. He sneaked to the corner, edging his head round the moonlit wall to see where they were going. It was immediately obvious. A gleaming car, Thanos' car, stood in the square, waiting in the shadow of the one plane tree. A man at the wheel. The men all climbed in, Thanos saying something brief to the driver. And the car purred out of the square, up a street on the far side leading to the outer part of the village and the road to Thanos' house. Pethi and Vleppo were left staring from the corner.

7

'Hello.' Tini, all shining fair in the sun, came round the stone wall of the garden. Jason, plumply smiling, came too.

'Dad's gone off to Piraeus, on the boat. He had to go to the bank in Athens. A telegram came. He'll be back tonight.'

'I know.' Pethi looked up from the tomato plants.

She gave a snort of exasperation. 'Everybody knows! Already this morning two neighbours asked me about it.'

Pethi laughed. 'Telegrams are events. Everyone on the island will have known every word of George's telegram before he did.'

It was so nearly true she forgave the exaggeration.

'What are you doing? Can I help?' She yanked Jason out of the vines and put him on a patch of stones next to Vleppo.

'In a minute you can give me a hand watering these tomatoes, but right now you can listen.'

He told it all, from the moment of wakening to Tini's dream voice, to Thanos' car gliding away with the sinister newcomers.

'Well . . . ' she said, as they faced each other across the row of plants. The cave voice . . . and Thanos? 'You don't think it was *all* a dream?' She hardly meant it, but it seemed worth checking.

Pethi's look was scathing. 'My mother heard me coming back. Wanted to know where I'd been.'

'So. What do you think?'

'What do *you* think?'

'It's to do with the mines?'

'It must be. Mustn't it? Silver, Thanos said.'

'But there's never been much silver here, has there?'

'Not what you'd call riches. That's what they said. "Riches".'

'Pethi!' A horrible thought. She whispered. 'Suppose Thanos has found something to do with the goddess. Some other ancient thing. Of silver, even. That would be riches, if he were selling in other countries. Heaven knows what he'd get for antiquities from Greece . . . '

Pethi was shocked. 'I didn't think of that.'

'Maybe that's why you were warned. The voice. Because of the goddess. Because of *her* riches.'

It was unbearable. Panic rose. Thanos . . . threatening their goddess. 'No. Oh, no.'

'Can't we tell the police?' Tini was desperate.

'A very clever idea,' scornfully, 'tell them Thanos brought friends here last night? Tell them about the cave?' He jabbed a stick into the ground. 'Anyway, we have one policeman. And he fears Thanos like everyone else.'

'Well then – why not telephone Athens? The Mining Company? At least find out what Thanos' plans are officially – '

'And every word we said to them would be known to Thanos within minutes.'

Of course. Tini was silenced.

Pethi sat on the stony soil, thoughtful. 'There's something

87

to do with the mines. I'm sure. Why sack all the men, otherwise? And the connection, between the voice, the goddess, and the mines – well, why shouldn't it just be Serifos? The life of the island. The jobs.' Surely the cave's secret was never meant to be revealed, and somehow the mines could be started again.

'It's important to you, the men's jobs.'

'Of course.' He looked surprised.

'I mean, more so. Since the cave. Otherwise you'd feel you must tell about the statue, so the men could work on a dig.'

It was so obvious Pethi didn't reply. But as he said nothing, Tini went on, drifting musingly among the vines:

'Although, maybe you'd rather not tell, ever. Even if the men have to leave the island.' She was turned away from Pethi, not seeing his face. 'Maybe even then, you'd feel it had to be a secret . . . would you?' She turned.

He stood white, shaking.

'Go away,' he said, not loudly. 'Go away from me.'

'Pethi . . . '

'Yesterday, you could see something. Today, you know nothing about me. Today, you're a blind, stupid *girl*.' The word was an insult. 'Go away – go!' He was shouting now. 'Go and tell everybody – why not?' He wheeled about, crashing through the plants, towards the house. Vleppo shot her a cold look and followed.

'Pethi! Pethi, I didn't mean . . . I was only thinking . . . '

He didn't turn.

*   *   *

Zoë stepped aboard the *Petros*.

'Dimitrios. What a job you've done.' She looked round the

painted deck, very serious. She watched Pethi unfurl the new red sails, making ready for the first trip.

Dimitrios, busy among ropes, kept his face turned away from Zoë, giving her privacy.

'It's different,' she said quietly, 'but the same too.'

She put down a basket of food, and ran a hand along the varnished edge of the cabin roof. Seeing her, Pethi was concerned; he forgot his hurt outrage at Tini that had given him a desperate need to escape, to sail in his boat, to fly out to sea.

At first Zoë had said no, she wouldn't come. And then had changed her mind without explanation. Perhaps because of her son, so anxious to sail in his new boat, the boat that had been his lost father's. Perhaps because she knew that sometime she must board the *Petros* again. Perhaps because she had had enough of the fidgety anxiety in the village.

Now, after a few minutes' stillness, she smiled a little. And, with sudden energy, began to help prepare the boat for the sail. Dimitrios grinned at Pethi's astonishment at her efficiency, her knowledge of seamanship: it had never occurred to him.

They went on wings out of the harbour mouth and towards the first cape. Pethi at the wheel leaned back to gaze in joy at the full, bright sails. 'She's a bird ... a bird ... ' he said softly. He looked briefly towards Zoë, almost smiled, and then swung his eyes back on course.

Zoë laughed a little. 'Yes, she's a bird.' Pethi looked like his father, black hair windblown. 'And you deserve her,' she added.

Pethi was happy. The *Petros* skimmed past the coastline of

cliffs, sun and wind in her sails. This was freedom, Happiness. Even Tini's words mattered less out here. He could even, almost, forget his twinge of guilt when Aspassia told him Tini had gone off walking with Jason, looking sad. So – she should have thought, before she spoke. No, it would not spoil this first wonderful sail in his own shining boat.

On they sailed. Past the end of the cape, Pethi was lured by the opening to a calm, blue bay. He brought the boat round to enter it, and in minutes the sails emptied of wind.

'Of course,' Dimitrios said at Pethi's grimace. 'These cliffs are huge. You are in the lee of them here.'

Pethi saw where he was. The bay was formed by two great cliffs . . . a vast cleft in the coastline. High above, his cave.

'Doesn't matter,' he said. 'It's a good place to bathe. And eat. Let's anchor.'

'D'you know that cave?' he asked Dimitrios a little later, through a mouthful of bread and olives.

Dimitrios shuddered. 'Bewitched. Every fisherman knows that.'

Zoë laughed, 'Bewitched!'

'It's as I say.' He saw nothing funny. 'Evil. Since ancient times, generations have known.'

Pethi stared at the cliffs, tracing the route he took from one to the other, seeing the ledges and footholds from a new viewpoint. The two platforms where the cliffs almost touched. The ledge running beneath the cave. Unless one already knew it was there, one would never guess. And then . . . Pethi screwed his eyes. Could it be?

'I'm swimming,' he announced, stripping to his pants. To

plunge over the side into the green glass depths, where rocks fathoms deep seemed clearly within touching distance, and fish shot by in orderly shoals. Pethi struck out for the base of the cliff.

Behind the first craggy rocks, he found a smooth stratum, almost a rock jetty. And yes . . . surely he had been right. From here ran a ledge, moving upwards. Could it lead to the cave? He was too near now to tell, but from the boat he was almost sure.

Glancing back to the *Petros*, he saw Dimitrios sitting smoking, facing out to sea. Zoë wasn't to be seen.

He started up the ledge. It was wide, and easy. Could people, in ancient times, have carried the statue up this way? Up and up. Now, he reckoned, he must be half way up to the cave. But the indentations of the cliff-face made it impossible to see. He climbed further. Now he was certain it must lead all the way, joining the ledge he usually followed to the cave. Why had he never noticed this from the cave itself? As far as he could remember, his ledge had ended just beyond the cave. Or had it? There was a jutting part of the cliff there, he visualized. Perhaps the ledge actually rounded this, only seeming to break off. It had never occurred to him, preoccupied with the cave, to look further.

A shout from below carried through the still air. He looked back, down to the *Petros*. How far away it looked, painted on the vivid bay. Tiny, unreal.

Dimitrios was waving both arms frantically, yelling. 'Come back, Pethi! Eh – come back you young fool!'

Zoë stood silently horrified.

* * *

91

Pethi heaved himself back on board, tossing a fish to Vleppo who waited in the shade. 'Don't fuss,' he said to his mother, 'it was perfectly safe.'

'Oh, perfectly,' Zoë was sardonic. 'A walk you'd take any day.' He grinned.

'Bah!' Dimitrios was all disapproval. 'Keep away from that place.'

'Why?'

'Others have tried to reach that cave, and been dashed from the cliffs by mysterious powers. That is what I know.' He put up a hand to stop Pethi speaking. 'It has been part of my family's land for generations. I know terrible stories.'

'On your land?'

'Certainly. You should know that.' He waved an arm. 'Up there, the mines. You know the disused one, the shaft by the old river bed. And not much further inland, the two iron mines that Thanos has closed.'

For no reason Pethi asked: 'The disused mine. Was that iron too?'

Dimitrios shrugged 'I don't remember. It was closed before I was born. Once my father had it investigated by experts, and he had some idea there could be silver there, or perhaps it was lead. Or both. There were some plans drawn, but I don't know what happened to them. Anyway, it must have been nonsense, for nothing was ever done.'

Pethi's heart lurched and hammered. Silver. Now he was sure. Thanos' dealings had to do with the mines. Not the goddess. He wished suddenly that Tini were there to share this marvellous relief.

He lay on his front on the sunlit deck, silent for some

time. Gradually, some of Dimitrios' words formed an idea.

'Dimitrios. Does it belong to Thanos, or to you, the land with the iron mines?' He didn't mention the third mine.

The fisherman shrugged. 'All of that part, it belongs to one of us. Or both. It is years since I saw the deeds.' Then he stared at Pethi. Something dawned. 'To one of us. Who knows? Yes indeed. Who knows?' He slapped his leg and laughed. Pethi laughed. Zoë stared at them.

'Come!' Dimitrios looked towards the afternoon sun. 'If I am to see my brother . . . '

'What?' Zoë cried.

'Maybe, maybe,' Dimitrios explained, '*I* myself own that land, with the mines.'

'And?'

'And maybe I can convince Thanos of it. Maybe I can discover if there's something going on. And maybe – '

'Maybe, maybe,' Zoë was impatient, 'maybe you're out of your mind. Maybe you'll tell me what you're talking about. Anyway, I thought you'd sold out your share when you left.'

'I sold nothing. I left, that is all. And I'll bet Thanos is as hazy about the deeds of our land as I am. So – think – if he says the mines are finished, useless, how can he complain if I want control of my land again. Eh? Eh?'

They all laughed as they sailed back towards the harbour.

Pethi remembered Thanos' words of the previous night. 'I'll come with you,' he casually offered Dimitrios. 'Then he won't be so suspicious, perhaps.'

* * *

Pethi's mind was spilling over with speculations as they

approached Thanos' house. The men that had come to the island. Mining experts, and workers, to get the silver? The plans that Dimitrios' and Thanos' father had made for the old mine – had Thanos found them again and so discovered "riches"? Had he, then, sacked all the men to work the silver mine himself, and sell the riches in some other country for huge profits? And with his mines officially closed, he would escape taxes. It began to look logical.

Hesitantly he said something of his thoughts to Dimitrios. He would have told about the men arriving on the previous night, but it was too complicated to explain why he himself had been by the harbour.

Dimitrios shook his head. 'A crazy idea,' he said. Then paused. 'Still, Pethi – as you say, it is logical. Perhaps it is true that Thanos has found some way of making money illegally through the mines. But without miners? How? And silver – ' he wagged his curly head again, ' – no, no. Not on Serifos.'

Thanos' house was large and white, standing alone outside the harbour village, built into the steep hillside. There were elegant arched doorways and windows, a paved courtyard, lavish tubs of flowers, and a huge wrought iron gateway.

The hunched little man guarding the gate was reluctant to let them in, but Dimitrios pushed past. 'That shows it,' he muttered to Pethi, 'he's up to no good. Not letting me in, his brother.'

Thanos appeared, frowning, across the courtyard.

'What do you want?' He flicked a sour look at Pethi. 'And why is he here?' Vleppo rumbled inwardly.

Dimitrios was all brotherliness. 'My friends,' he said, 'were

94

coming this way with me, that's all. I wanted to make a small request, Thanos. Have you a moment?'

Thanos jiggled amber beads, suspicious. 'Don't start any of your – '

'It is business. Very simple. A friendly suggestion.' Dimitrios smiled, relaxed. 'Why don't we sit down . . . ?'

Impatiently Thanos waved his brother towards some white-painted chairs at the corner of the courtyard. He made no offer of hospitality; anybody else would have called for coffee. Pethi sat down, Vleppo beside him, without being asked. He looked casually round the courtyard, at the windows of the house, as if totally bored by what the men were saying. Nobody could be seen. Except, once – briefly, a woman's face at a high window. Damia? It could have been; she looked young enough. Nobody ever saw Thanos' woman in the village.

'Well?' Thanos waited.

'Quite simply, brother,' Dimitrios said cheerfully, 'it's about the mines. And my friends.'

Thanos sneered. 'If you've come to plead for your friends' jobs, don't waste my time. The mines are finished.' He stood up as if to dismiss them.

But Dimitrios nodded. 'I'm sure you're right,' he said.

'What?'

'I understand,' Dimitrios assured him. 'For you, there would be no profit. The Mining Company is no longer interested. Fine. But what about this – *I* would like to run the mines. I would like to buy you out.'

Thanos stared at him. 'YOU! You own nothing.'

Dimitrios shook his head, very patiently. 'On the contrary Thanos. The land where those two iron mines are does in fact belong to me. Evidently you don't remember how the land was divided in our father's will.' He looked at his brother blandly. 'They are mine. I am coming to you only as a matter of form – of course, I will make you some payment if you wish, as I said, to buy you out, to compensate you for your hard work –'

Thanos was banging the table. 'YOU ARE LYING!' he shrieked, purple-faced.

'If you would like to see the deeds . . . '

'YOU ARE LYING! You are playing games. There is something you know –'

'Know?'

Thanos might have murdered him. 'You are trying to ruin me!' he shouted.

'But Thanos – how can I ruin you? As you have said yourself, there is no more work in the mines. You would gain by selling to me. As for myself, I want no profit. Only to cover costs, for my friends to have jobs.' He shrugged innocently.

Thanos was breathing deeply. 'I shall speak to my lawyer in Athens tonight. I shall telephone. And check on these deeds.'

Dimitrios was politely helpful. 'I have a copy,' he lied. 'I can show you them this evening if you wish.'

Thanos choked. 'Get out!' he almost screamed. 'You would try to ruin my plans . . . ' He stopped.

Dimitrios looked at him. 'Plans, brother? What plans are these?' And then, remembering his conversation with Pethi, he went a step too far. 'Plans for riches for yourself, perhaps? Eh, Thanos? Plans which mean you don't want anyone near those mines?'

Pethi was certain that if he had not been there Thanos might

96

have killed Dimitrios. As it was, he seized him by the throat and dragged him to his feet: it wasn't difficult, Dimitrios being a small man.

'Be careful, my brother,' he said, quietly now. 'Be careful. You are playing dangerous games. And listen. If anyone is seen on that land – my land – unauthorized, they won't get off it alive.' He flicked a look towards Pethi. 'Do you hear that Dimitrios? You, or any of your friends.' He let go of Dimitrios, who rubbed his throat painfully.

'You are a fool, Thanos,' he said unemotionally. 'You have let power make you a fool.' He took Pethi's arm and they walked out of the courtyard, Vleppo following.

Thanos, watching them go, spat. Then turned to the house. He had arrangements to make.

8

Tini walked slowly between the tamarisk trees at the harbour's edge, heading for Tassos' café where she could watch for the evening steamer's arrival. And her father.

She was reluctant, strangely, to move into the bright lights of the café. Another day she would have enjoyed it, an adventure of experimenting with the language, and revelling in the courteous attention and service. Today she was depressed, unhappy.

She leaned on a tree and looked into the nothingness of a darkening sky. How stupid she had been to say that to Pethi; to imply that he would let his island suffer rather than reveal the statue in the cave. Their goddess. And how angry he had been, hating her. After yesterday, when everything had been shared, and mysterious, and happy too.

Then there were all her confused thoughts about the island. The poverty, the mines closing, and Thanos. What could they do about Thanos? They were helpless. Surely all they could do to help the island was to tell her father about the statue – to give Serifos back its goddess and some hope for work. The island was dying, that was what they all said, the groups of black-clad old ladies.

But the mystery of the cave – they would lose that. She didn't want to lose it, any more than Pethi. Even though it had been frightening, inexplicable, when they had talked about it afterwards. Still, it had been magical. And the voice in the night – her voice – speaking to Pethi. Leading him to Thanos . . .

She had come in a circle of thoughts.

Tini blinked in the bright lights of Tassos' café. Unconsciously she had drifted through the trees towards it, and now stood looking stupidly at the tables. Tassos saw her, and hurried to greet her.

'*Kalyspéra*, good evening, my little flower,' he said, as if they hadn't met for months. His beaming face made her feel happier immediately. One of his strong, boiling cups of coffee would make her feel better still.

Not many people were at the café. A few groups of men, talking quietly. There was a gloom, quite apart from her own mixed thoughts. Even the lean cats slunk more warily, it seemed. Sipping her coffee from its miniscule cup, Tini felt a sudden, intense sense of loss. She knew, really, that they would have to give up their secret, she and Pethi. Their goddess. And now . . . would they never know what the strange words had meant? What the mystery was that involved them?

'You are very thoughtful, our little newcomer to Serifos.' The voice was rich and beautiful, speaking slowly and musically.

Tini looked up. A priest, the *pappas*, towered. He smiled. Tini was so absorbed in this straight, black-robed figure, with bushy beard and stove-pipe hat, an incredibly handsome face and lively eyes, that she said nothing.

'May I sit with you?'

She nodded. And smiled. 'I'm sorry. I was thinking.'

'As I noticed.'

'You're a friend of Pethi.' Tini waved a hand in the direction of the greenly-gleaming cats' eyes. 'He told me you were once a vet.'

'Yes. Ridiculous isn't it?' He gave a grin that Tini wouldn't have associated with a priest. 'And you are Tini, from London. And I guess you are awaiting your father.'

Tini laughed. 'I suppose everyone knows exactly why he went into Athens?'

'To the bank, wasn't it?' The *pappas* chuckled at her face. 'You'll get used to it,' he said, and called to Tassos for an *ouzo*. 'Life here is poor, and you strangers are wonderful news. Greeks are curious anyway of course, every one of us, but –' he smiled, ' – you can't blame us being especially curious about people from London coming here to live. Perhaps it's a wish to share in your life. A form of love.'

'Oh.' Tini felt vaguely ashamed of her irritation that morning when everyone had known about the telegram.

'Another coffee?' As Tassos' young son brought his *ouzo*. 'The boat is late of course.'

'Yes please.' Tini watched this young, bearded priest drink his strong liquor. 'I can't imagine,' she said, 'the vicars at home sitting in a café drinking *ouzo*. People would write to *The Times*.'

'More's the pity, perhaps,' he said. 'Now – why are you looking so sad? Disillusioned so soon about our island?'

The *pappas*, if anyone, Tini thought, would probably understand something of the mystery of the cave. Intuitively. Maybe some day she could tell him.

'Not really,' she answered him. 'But there are many things

to *be* sad about here, aren't there? But I'm not complaining,' quickly, 'because I love Serifos. I love it. I even feel I belong here, especially – '

He looked at her. 'Don't worry,' he said calmly, drinking the last of his *ouzo*. 'I'm sure you'll come to the right decision.'

Tini's head shot up in amazement. How did he know there was a decision to make?

'Here comes Pethi,' he said, getting up. 'I'll leave you to talk.' Before she could voice a thought he was on his feet, loftily, and moving away. Then he turned: 'I'll let you know what my plans are for the cats,' he grinned, and went. She watched his straight black back, feeling she had been visited by some mischievous thought-reader.

'So you met our *pappas*.' Pethi sat down. Vleppo smoothed himself warmly against Tini's legs.

She said feebly: 'He seems to read minds.' Pethi looked excited, she thought. Bright-eyed. But not angry.

'Pethi . . . '

'It's all right.'

'I'm sorry. It was stupid. I didn't even believe it – I think it was really that *I* didn't want to tell about the goddess, no matter what,' she gabbled.

'It's all right, I said. Forget it.' He smiled. 'I'm sorry I got angry.' They both felt a vast relief. Pethi picked up her coffee cup and took a sip. 'And now, listen.'

She soon saw that his excitement was a mass of ideas, discoveries, plans. He told her about the afternoon, the sail to the bay, Dimitrios' casual information about the mines, his own suspicions about the silver. The new way to the cave. The visit to Thanos' house. The anger. Thanos being certain that

Dimitrios knew something – but what? The danger, with Thanos forewarned. The mine area, the clifftops, guarded.

'What will he do?' Tini quavered.

'He has men, we know that. And guns. I told you he likes shooting. Whatever he's up to he must have a lot to lose – you should've seen how furious he was. He meant what he said.'

'He wouldn't . . . *kill.*'

'Yes. He would.' There seemed nothing more to say. Tini shivered, unable to believe. The clifftop guarded with guns. The cave now inaccessible.

'What then?'

Pethi leaned across the table. 'First, if there *is* silver in that mine, there's work for Serifos. Right? Somehow we've got to get someone from the Mining Company here, to investigate. Second, it might be an idiotic idea, like Dimitrios said. There might *not* be silver, and whatever Thanos' plans are there might not actually be any work for the men, in any of the mines.'

'And?' Tini felt nervous.

'It's obvious, isn't it? We have to tell. We have to.' Pethi thumped the table as if he were annoyed. 'Otherwise, it's all wrong. Even if there's mining work, there might not be enough for everyone. And if George could get started, they'd have a choice of jobs, and . . . oh, well.' He stared out to the harbour. Tini had a hideous feeling she might cry.

'There are the lights of the steamer,' he said.

'But, our goddess – ' she managed.

Pethi looked back at her. 'You decided too, though, didn't you? That we should tell.'

'But I thought you'd talk me out of it.'

Pethi caught hold of her hand, not caring about curious

smiling glances. 'You were thinking, if they take the goddess' head from the cave, the mystery might vanish?'

'Yes! How do we know – the words, whatever they were, might never happen again. And they might tell us . . . well, it can't be for *nothing*, can it? It's too strange. We might lose it. For ever.' Tini's face was tragic.

The lights of the steamer were nearer.

'And with Thanos' men there –' she went on. 'Unless –' seizing the idea, 'we went by the new way, from the bay.'

'No.' He pulled her up, to walk along the quay. 'The boat would be seen. Listen. There's only one thing, if you agree. We go the usual way to the cave. We try and see if the words happen again. We record them.'

'What? How?'

The steamer chugged down the harbour.

'Tassos will help. Electric gadgets are his hobby. He said he'd lend me a small tape-recorder. I didn't have to say why, luckily. Don't you see – if we've *got* the words, somebody – George – might be able to tell what they say . . . '

They were running now. The steamer was almost at the pier. Villagers converged on it.

'But it's impossible. The men –'

'They won't be there till morning. We'll go tonight. Tonight. And tomorrow, we can tell George about it all.'

'Tonight!' Tini came to a standstill and several people barged into her. 'In the dark!'

'It'll be all right. Come on – let's meet George. He might have some ideas on the mining thing.'

Tini's mind reeled. The cliff, in the dark.

Passengers and islanders fell over themselves, goats, parcels and feet as the gangway was let down. George materialized suddenly behind a fat woman carrying three suitcases with unlikely strength. Vleppo stood back, out of reach of the feet, the hooves, the bleating and calling.

George's eyes were shining as he met them. He gave them no chance to speak.

'Guess who I ran into in Amalias Avenue,' he said. 'Sir Rolf. Imagine that.'

'Who?' Pethi scooped Vleppo up from the crowd.

'Sir Rolf Roller,' Tini explained. 'An archaeologist. Quite famous in Britain.'

'Old friend. More than that – my teacher,' George said, striding out energetically. 'We had lunch. I was telling him about the island. He got quite fascinated by my ideas. Said that if I ever got on to anything, he'd pull the strings and get things moving fast. How about that?'

Pethi and Tini looked at each other. 'Marvellous,' Tini said.

'It'd save months.' George was pleased. 'And the news at the bank was good, by the time they'd sorted out various messages from London. Some more royalties on the books. So I got us some lamb chops for dinner, lots of them. Let's all eat together at our house.'

'All right,' Tini said. 'Then we can tell you our news, maybe.'

George was surprised. 'Has something happened?'

* * *

They all leaned back after the feast of lamb chops grilled with herbs, and a salad concocted by Zoë out of green vegetables that George claimed would have been dismissed as weeds in England. They were delicious.

'So,' Pethi finished telling George about developments with Thanos, 'he thinks we know something. So he'll be watching us. All of us.'

'Damn,' George said. 'If only I'd thought, I could've called into the Mining Company offices today and got some facts.'

'No,' Dimitrios shook his head. 'Why should they tell you anything? Besides, I'm sure Thanos has it all tied up. No doubt the Mining Company is fully convinced the iron mines are finished.'

'What about the silver?'

'If that's so . . . then he's kept it to himself. But no, no.' Dimitrios couldn't believe it. 'That can't be Thanos' plan.'

'Why not?' Zoë protested. 'Whatever it is, it must be worth a lot to Thanos.'

'Especially,' Pethi put in, 'if he's planning to sell somewhere outside Greece, and avoid taxes here.'

'All right,' George said, pondering. 'We know he's up to something, and you think it must be to do with the mines. And, after all, what else could it be about?' Pethi and Tini were careful not to look at each other. 'And he thinks Dimitrios knows what. What can he do? What's his next likely move, apart from watching his land?'

'He'd kill me if he could,' Dimitrios said.

'But – he's your brother!' Tini cried.

'That means nothing to Thanos, my little angel.'

Zoë and Aspassia nodded. Thanos would do anything. George spread his fingers thoughtfully on the table.

'Would the Mining Company listen to you, Dimitrios, if you went there, and explained your suspicions?'

'Of course. They know me. But it's impossible for me to speak to them, if Thanos is to be watching me –'

'And you're taking your boats out to fish tonight as usual?'

'Certainly.' Then George's words struck Dimitrios. He grinned. 'Ah! At least – I can appear to go fishing, can I not?'

Everyone saw, and laughed. Dimitrios should make for Piraeus and Athens, after setting out as usual in his fishing caique.

'And Thanos would suspect nothing,' Tini said. 'That's brilliant.'

'Perfect,' Pethi said. 'Why didn't we think of it before?'

'I must go alone,' Dimitrios murmured. 'But I can organize that. Nobody must know, even my nearest friends.' He nodded, forming plans. 'Yes, it will work.' His face was bright, glad to be able to do something about the miners' problems. 'I can be there in the morning, and back by evening.'

*   *   *

They were over the ridge on the stony mule-track with the windmills behind them before Pethi spoke.

'All right?'

'Yes. No. I'm scared.'

'Look at the moon. It's like daylight. You needn't worry – it'll be just like when you climbed the first time. Only easier, because you've done it once.'

'I suppose so.'

They scrambled over rocks, leaving the quiet village behind.

The island seemed empty, here on the bare hillside, the moon filling the sky with light.

'Did you get the tape-recorder?'

'Yes. It's easy.' Pethi held up a duffel-bag he carried. 'You just push a button.'

'What if it doesn't happen? If the words don't come?'

Pethi said nothing for a few moments as they trudged down a valley, Vleppo a shadow beside them.

'Well, if they don't, at least we'll know we're not losing anything when the statue's taken out of the cave.'

Another ten minutes walking, climbing over rock ridges, and the old river-bed, dry since ancient times, was ahead of them.

'Thanos' land,' Pethi whispered. 'Watch for any movement or light.'

Tini's heart seemed deafening.

'D'you think there'll be someone here already?'

'No. But just in case.'

They crept on, feeling dangerously exposed in the moonlight. Anyone who was about, Pethi realized, would almost certainly see them first. There were few shadows to hide in, once away from the rutted shelter of the river-bed.

They crawled up the last few metres of the next ridge: ahead of them, the cliff-top. Behind and to their left, out of sight, the disused mine. Lying on the stony ground, they peered all round. There was no movement.

Pethi grabbed Tini's hand. 'Ready?'

'Yes.' Quick, she thought, before I change my mind.

They ran forward, keeping low. Vleppo ran with them, eyes gleaming. Crouching at the cliff's edge, Pethi said:

'Go on, Vleppo. I'm not carrying you tonight.'

The cat's eyes flicked upwards to Pethi's face, then, sleekly, Vleppo jumped down to the first ledge. Quickly, Pethi followed. His face was in shadow as he looked up at Tini, his hair edged with moon silver. 'We'll take it easy,' he said calmly, as Tini stood trembling. 'I'll tell you as we go. Now, don't start until I say. I'll get as far as the first good-sized ledge.' His head disappeared.

Alone, Tini almost panicked. The whole idea of the climb was terrifying: the sheer black drop. She could slip. Easily. A loose stone. Her stomach lurched. She would be sick, she was sure.

'All right.' Pethi's voice, low and clear. 'It's all firm.' As if he had read her mind.

She took huge breaths, glancing wildly around her. Then stepped to the first ledge. Not far below her, Pethi's head was a black shock of hair. Vleppo was out of sight. She wouldn't look down. Down there where the cliff fell far far away to the foaming sea.

At the last second, before her head ducked below the cliff-edge, she thought she saw a light: was it? The flicker of something, perhaps in the direction of the old mine. She dismissed it as nerves, or the moon reflecting on something shiny.

'Just like daylight,' Pethi said confidently as she joined him on the first big ledge. 'You can see perfectly. Just concentrate on your hands, and feel with your feet. Easy isn't it?' He was completely at ease, familiar with this plunging cliff, grinning at her moon-pale face. 'Now, we go straight down again, remember, five or six long steps. Take it slowly.' He led the way.

Jaw clenched, Tini followed. She kept her eyes fixed on her hands, clinging to the rock face. It was, as Pethi had said, like daylight. It was silly to be afraid: the first time she had come, the sun had shone, but she doubted if she had seen much more clearly.

'And now,' Pethi said when she caught him up again, 'this ledge. It goes quite a way, moving down to our right – under the overhanging cliff. See?' Tini peered along the lit-up cliff-face. The huge dark bulge of rock leaned into the sky.

They edged, hugging the cliff. Pethi called back from moment to moment, warning of unexpected dips or crags, or encouraging her when the ledge narrowed.

The next section was easier again. The ledge was broader, descending in short steps. Footholds were firm and deep. But once, a cloud flicked across the moon.

'Oh!' Tini stopped. Fear rose. 'It's pitch black. It's pitch black.'

They waited, clinging like flies on a wall. It was for only a few seconds, but for Tini they were long and dark, with the black sea sounding far below. Then the night was brilliant again.

At last, the natural platform, reaching out to its partner on the opposite cliff. They sat for a few moments, next to the waiting Vleppo.

'That's the worst over,' Pethi said, hearing Tini let out a long breath.

'What, though, if there'd been no moon?'

He shrugged. 'There is. So why worry?' He would have wanted to come anyway, she knew. 'Ready?' he asked.

They stepped from one side to the other, across the chasm,

high above the jagged rocks where the sea hurled and boomed.

The ledge to the cave was almost straightforward after their descent. Though no wider than the length of a man's foot, it was level and direct. They hauled themselves into the cave mouth; Vleppo was there in a vertical spring.

'Look.' Pethi was pointing further along the ledge. 'Now you can see why we'd never have known there was another way up.'

The ledge appeared to stop abruptly, broken, a sheer edge. But, they now realized, it actually turned a corner of the cliff; only when seen from below, as Pethi had done, was it possible to tell that the ledge continued.

They went slowly, oddly nervous, down into the cave, nearer and nearer to the marble head of the goddess. Down, down, went the tunnel, the beam of Pethi's torch licking on the rocks.

'How d'you feel?' Pethi asked at the cavern of stalactites.

'All right. I think. But it's starting, very faintly. A kind of ringing in my ears, only not quite – in the back of my mind, almost.'

Pethi put an arm round her shoulders gently. 'I think it will work,' he said, and led her through to the cave of the goddess.

Without pausing, they moved towards the centre, where the face of this remote, beautiful woman looked up into the torchlight. Vleppo's eyes shone beside her. Tini could feel Pethi's arm, strong round her shoulders, extraordinarily clearly. Again the sensation of her skin ice-cool, her hair floating. The humming, distant voices, faraway, in her brain.

'Sit here, and be comfortable.' Pethi was assured, and in

command. He helped her, firmly. 'Now wait, while I get the tape-recorder ready.'

He took it from the duffel-bag, a compact little machine, and placed it on the smooth cave floor, beside the sculpted marble head. The microphone was put right next to Tini. He moved quickly and neatly: once more he felt that nothing was impossible.

Tini sat, feeling herself to be in the centre of a strange and immense peacefulness and power, waiting. She was no longer nervous. Pethi switched on the recorder. 'Ready?' he whispered. Tini nodded, and again, high above them, they heard the little owl shriek. Tini's eyes seemed to be flashing blue light as she looked at Pethi, and then down at the goddess. She reached out her hands.

There was silence in the cave. Pethi waited, unmoving. Vleppo stared at Tini. Tini herself felt the distant humming sensation fill her body, quietly, slowly. And then she lost all awareness.

This time the voice began in a murmur. So quiet that Pethi could hardly hear; he was sure the microphone would pick nothing up. The words were slow at first, and then, gradually they gathered speed and volume. Tini gazed straight ahead, her vivid eyes in trance, now talking clearly and rapidly. Pethi tried to follow, to catch a word or two, but couldn't. He hardly dared breathe, so fearful was he of breaking this mysterious flow . . . what did it mean? Was it a message from the past, or something they must know now? Or would it, in the end, mean nothing?

Tini's voice paused slightly. She made a slight moan, leaning her head back, shaking it from side to side slowly, her gaze turned up into the darkened chimney of the cave. Then she spoke again, very slowly, with an air of lament. Her hair waved back and forth, spun silver. Pethi heard again the ancient words for shield, and snakes, and then . . . was it? The word for 'owl'. Yes, owl. She repeated it. Pethi was sure. After that, he lost the words. Even if he had known them, Tini's speech was far too quick; her head was bent again, and she gazed straight into the marble face of the goddess. The voice was clear, staccato, even vehement. The words filled the cave, filled Pethi with a strength that was exhilarating. Vleppo sat motionless, his yellow eyes fixed, enthralled, upon Tini's face.

She must have been talking for fifteen minutes. Pethi watched her pale face, saw shadows under her eyes. Should he end it – lift her hands from the marble and 'wake' her? Or would she stop, anyway, after a while? But perhaps she wouldn't stop. Pethi battled inwardly. Tini looked exhausted.

'What should I do . . . Zeus, what should I do?' Amazed, he realized he had murmured aloud, calling on Zeus, father of the ancient gods. And in the next second, Tini's words ended in a way that left him trembling. She gave a terrible, high, unbelievable scream.

Her eyes were still fixed on the sculpted face. And across that face, Pethi saw, crawling over the marble forehead, was a black spider. It moved slowly, its ugly legs contrasting grotesquely with the smooth whiteness. Pethi was frozen, shocked by the scream from Tini.

A large black paw darted out: Vleppo. With a cat's swiftness, he smacked down with all the force of his large foot upon the spider, and in the same movement had scooped it away, dashing it across the cave. Then, as if nothing had happened, he looked up again at Tini. There was a second's pause, and she lifted her hands from the goddess and looked, bewildered, at Pethi. He pushed the button on the tape-recorder.

'What happened? Something startled me.'

'A spider. It crawled over her.'

'A spider?'

'Vleppo got it.'

'A *spider*. I'm not frightened of spiders.'

'Well, you were then.'

'How peculiar.' Tini got up, stretching her arms. 'Did I say anything?' She only just dared to ask. 'Did it work?'

'You talked for easily fifteen minutes.'

'That long! Did you get it all?' She stared at the little tape-recorder with a kind of awe.

'All of it. I couldn't understand though. Snakes and shield again. And this time, "glavx". Owl.'

'Owl? Owl! Of course.'

He realized too. 'Athene's bird, the owl. It's on the ancient coins. And – why didn't I think of that? I always hear the little owl in the cave, and that night by the harbour . . . '

'It all means something, Pethi. It must.'

They were exhausted. They moved to the side of the cave to sit leaning against a smooth part of its wall. Pethi, who had had little sleep the previous night, could have slept now in an instant. Tini yawned; the sounds had gone from her head now. Only emptiness was left, tired emptiness.

'Let's eat something.' Pethi dug into the canvas bag again. 'I thought we might need it, not getting any sleep.'

Tini watched, eyebrows up, as he brought out a hunk of cheese, some bread, and a few tomatoes.

'I suspect you of genius,' she sighed. 'Any minute now you'll produce a cup of coffee.'

'Lemonade,' he grinned, bringing out a bottle. 'From Tassos.'

They ate, feeling better with every moment.

'Is George's classical Greek good?' Pethi asked.

'I've heard people say so. I wouldn't know. But he has done translations, and he can actually speak it.'

'It'll need to be good. You spoke terrifically fast at times.'

They sat silently; there was too much to think about. And, hardly realizing it, they dozed.

Then, suddenly, Tini said: 'It must be getting light.'

The faintest of grey lights was filtering down the cave's chimney. Pethi leapt up, cramming the remains of the food and then the tape-recorder into the bag. 'We've been out hours. I should have realized. Not leaving the village until well after midnight, and the climb took longer than usual. Come on – we must be away from here before Thanos is up.'

With only one swift glance back at the soft gleam of the goddess' face, they hurried out of the cave, across the cavern of stalactites, and up into the dark tunnel. At last, they were in the entrance cave. Outside the sky was pearl-grey as dawn arrived. One or two bright stars still showed.

'We should start at once,' Pethi said, 'if you're all right.'

'I'm fine. Anyway, it's getting light so fast. We can't wait.'

'Don't hurry. We'll go as we came – slowly. Once we're at the top of the cliff again the sun will be up, and we'll watch out for anybody. Just in case.'

'Go ahead then. I'll be right behind.'

Pethi fixed the duffel-bag over his shoulder and stepped to

the cave mouth, Vleppo with him. Far below him the sea shone, limpid. The grey light of dawn was beginning to have a hint of blue. The cliffsides brightened.

Then Pethi gasped and shot back into the cave as if he had been struck, dragging Vleppo with him.

'What? What is it?' Tini saw his shocked face.

'Up the cliff. Men.'

'Oh no.'

'Three, I saw. Holy mother of god. Already. What are they doing there? Exactly where we go up.'

'Thanos' men?'

'Who else?'

It was horrifying.

'Let me look.' Tini crept forward to peer one-eyed out of the cave. The opposite cliff rose high: she could see the ledges they had followed in the moonlight, now lit more and more brightly by the dawn. At the top of the cliff, only a short way from their starting point, she could see a man, walking slowly. Like a sentry. He was carrying a rifle.

9

'I can see one. Now another, talking to him. Pointing. Oh, here comes the third. Pethi – '

'Keep back. What?'

'They've got guns. Big ones. Rifles I think.'

'Oh *god*.'

Tini drew in her head. 'Surely they can't know we're here?'

Pethi hunched, frowning. 'Maybe somebody saw us last night, at the clifftop. We would have been clearly visible in that moon. But even then, they wouldn't know we'd gone to the cave.'

Tini remembered the flicker of light, hardly there, as she had stood at the first ledge. She told Pethi.

'That could be it then,' he muttered. 'They might know somebody was about, and they don't know if they're still about. Thanos must have put them on watch, in case.'

'Or maybe they're just keeping guard generally, only earlier than we expected.'

'Maybe.' Pethi doubted it.

'Couldn't we get to the platform part without them seeing us – take a chance – and climb the cliff. Then run for it?' Tini suggested wildly.

Pethi was all scorn. 'Run for it? Faster than a bullet, I

suppose? And don't suggest we go out with our hands up, saying we were just out for an early walk.' He was relentless. 'Think. Thanos associates me with Dimitrios knowing something. We're perched on a high cliff. Thanos, whatever it is he's planning, isn't going to let us get in his way. Why, otherwise, put three big men on guard?'

Tini leant against the side of the cave, silent, determined that her tears of fatigue and fear wouldn't win. Only days ago, unbelievably, she had been safely in grey, damp Notting Hill, with Serifos a romantic fantasy. And at that first thrilling view of the island, white houses on bare rock against blue sky, every outline pure in the clear sun . . . how could she have suspected this terror, men waiting to kill, as they were trapped in a cliff that plunged sheer to disaster?

Pethi looked at her remorsefully. 'Sorry,' he mumbled. 'It was my first thought, too, to risk it. But they could just pick us off the cliff. Anything. Who'd ever know what had really happened?'

Tini shrugged jerkily. 'So we wait.'

They sat down, suddenly waif-like, near each other. For some time they were silent, thinking. Outside the day brightened.

'I'll have another look.' As Pethi spoke Vleppo also crept forward; together they craned out warily, and the cat made a faint spitting noise. Tini knew what Pethi would say.

'Thanos is there.'

'Doing what?'

'Talking. Waving his arms around. Seems to be angry. He's telling them to spread out, spacing them along the cliff.' Pethi watched. 'Now he's going. And they're staying.' He sounded very tired. 'Hell. Somebody must have seen us, even if they don't know exactly where we went.'

He came back to join Tini. 'You go to sleep. Look, we'll move along here, and I can still see out by moving my head. Lean on me.' He resettled Tini, putting an arm round her shoulders. The rock floor wasn't comfortable, but they were too tired to complain. 'We'll just have to wait until it's dark again.'

'But Dad. And Zoë. They'll go out of their minds.'

'I know.' Pethi thought of his mother, probably now, finding that Aphrodite hadn't been milked, wondering where he was. 'I should've left a note. In case. Didn't think.'

Tini sat upright again, her voice rising. 'And if we wait until night – what if the men stay there, and – '

'Don't forget Dimitrios. He'll be back, with help, or information. Something, anyway, to deal with Thanos.' Surely Thanos couldn't keep his men up there if some official from the Mining Company came to investigate . . .

'Dimitrios! I'd forgotten. Oh, I hope everything went all right for him.'

*　　*　　*

Dimitrios sang.

No doubt, the plan had worked excellently. He and his fishermen had set off after the usual preparations of nets and lines.

The men that always accompanied him on his own caique were with him again, including his oldest friend Pavlos. Nobody watching from the quay could possibly have guessed that this departure of the little fleet was any different.

The boats had moved from the harbour in a slow chain of lights. Possibly Dimitrios had been more tense and thoughtful than usual, but none of the men would have noticed. They were too busy . . . and besides, it was impossible not to be thoughtful, the troubles of Serifos being as they were.

Beyond the harbour mouth, the boats reached the point where they would separate, spreading out for the night's fishing. It was now that Dimitrios surprised his crew by hailing the nearest caique to come alongside. He told Pavlos and the rest of his men to change vessels, leaving him alone on his own boat.

'Tell nobody, Pavlos,' he said rapidly and with authority, 'but I must go alone to Piraeus. I have business to attend to. You are in charge.' His friend stared. The other fishermen murmured, astonished. Dimitrios had never been known to leave the fishing fleet. Although the boss, he always liked to be involved, to work along with his men.

'Are you mad?' Pavlos asked him. 'Tonight the catch will be good, surely.'

Dimitrios smiled. 'Yes, yes. But this is important – vital. Just believe that. I'll be back tomorrow as usual.' Their curious faces watched him. 'And I'll explain. But say nothing, to anyone.'

His men nodded, and left his caique. He trusted them, and they all trusted Dimitrios. They knew too that this extraordinary move of his must be to do with the mining and that evil brother Thanos. Why otherwise would he wait until away from the watchful harbour before sending them from his caique?

He waved as they pulled away. Then, with a huge breath of

relief, he restarted his engine and swung round on course for Piraeus, the port of Athens. It had worked. Thanos could not know.

Dimitrios looked up at the moon and stars as Pethi and Tini looked at them on the ridge beyond the windmills. The night was beautiful. His hands steered his ship lightly and surely. Tomorrow, Thanos would be shown for what he was. At last. Whatever he was doing, he could not continue in the face of the authorities, that was certain. And, with luck, Dimitrios' friends might regain some of their mining jobs.

The lights of his fishing fleet had faded to tiny fireflies behind him now. Gradually, they disappeared completely. Over on the starboard side he could see the lights of the island Kythnos floating by, a village or two showing like a scattering of gold-dust. The night breeze was cold and fresh. Free, he was free. And he would help his island.

Dimitrios began to sing. He sang the old songs he had learned on Serifos, songs which began generations ago; those that the men in tavernas would dance to when the mood possessed them. They were filled with profound joy, and inexpressible sorrow.

The engine was vibrating noisily, and Dimitrios' voice was richly vigorous. It was impossible for him to have heard somebody creep from the cabin behind him. But a man's dark outline emerged, slowly, menacingly. For a second or two it stood behind Dimitrios, waiting. And then, with all the success of speed and surprise, brought a fishing-net over Dimitrios' head, and down, pinning his arms. The engine was stopped.

Alone out there on the sea it would hardly have mattered that

Dimitrios' shouts were loud and his struggles violent. Nevertheless they lasted only seconds. A terrible blow made vivid lights inside his brain. And then . . . nothing.

*   *   *

'Awake?'

Tini uncricked her neck from Pethi's shoulder.

'How long've I been asleep?'

'Two hours maybe. The sun's moved round.'

'You must be in agony, leaning on that rock.'

'I'm all right.' They shifted stiff limbs.

'Anything happen?'

'Thanos came back again.' Pethi was worried.

'And?'

'He was cheerful. Laughing, in fact. Slapping his men on the back. They were laughing too. I don't know exactly why, but it was sinister.'

'Sinister?' Tini felt cold.

'As if . . . he'd scored some point or other. I don't know.'

'Maybe he'd just had a good breakfast.' As a joke it didn't come off. They sat quietly for some moments.

'I've thought about us getting out of here.'

'Tonight, you mean.'

'Yes, but . . . look, we ought to have some alternative ideas. Our first plan didn't work out exactly right, did it? We ought to reckon on something else going wrong. Like Dimitrios being held up in Athens, not getting back in time. We can't stay here another night. For one thing, we've got hardly any food.'

'What else can we do?' Tini felt panic in her stomach.

'Well, I was thinking of the goddess' cave. Where it goes high up, the opening. Daylight comes in there.'

'We'd never climb up that! Are you mad? Think how far it must go – right up to the clifftop, presumably. And it begins lower down than this cave. That's crazy.'

'Probably. But Vleppo could, I think.'

Tini stared at Pethi, and then at the snoozing cat.

'Vleppo . . . ?'

'And take a message. To my mother. They wouldn't see him.'

It didn't seem possible. Tini said: 'A message? Would he know how?'

Vleppo opened one golden eye and looked at her.

'Of course. We could tie a note. If it's impossible to climb, we'll have to forget it. But it's worth trying, isn't it?'

Pethi's eyes were bright. There was hope again. It was a superb idea.

'Yes, oh yes!' Tini said. 'But what would you say – what would you tell Zoë?'

'The *Petros*.'

'What?'

'The way down to the sea.'

'The *Petros*!' Tini seized Pethi's arm. 'That's brilliant. Oh, that really is. We'd go down the cliff tonight – yes?'

He nodded. Neither of them mentioned the men at the clifftop with guns: as an escape route it would be horribly dangerous. Still, darkness would be some cover. Pethi said:

'Ideally, we'd start before the moon was properly up.'

Tini said nothing. He was right. But an unknown path . . . in moonless dark.

Pethi said: 'It's all right. This is only if Dimitrios gets held up. We probably won't have to do it.' But recalled Thanos on the clifftop, laughing, successful, and felt afraid.

'Let's do the note.' Tini was going through her pockets for stray paper, and found a scrap.

Pethi wrote. 'This all right?' he asked and read out: 'SAFE IN CAVE BUT GUARDED. IF DIMITRIOS DELAYED BRING PETROS AFTER DARK BEFORE MOON TO CAVE BAY AND WAIT. VLEPPO WILL BRING RETURN MESSAGE. PETHI, TINI.'

'Fine.'

They made a collar for Vleppo from the leather strap on the tape-recorder, fixing the note to it with a hairpin from another of Tini's pockets. The cat sat patiently.

'You stay here,' Pethi said to Tini, 'and watch. Anyway, you'll only start feeling peculiar again if you come down with me.'

'All right.'

'I'm going to try climbing up a bit myself to see what it's like, so don't worry if I'm a good while.'

She nodded, and stroked Vleppo's wise black head. 'Be careful,' she told him, thinking in fear of the guns.

'He will be.' Boy and cat vanished into the darkness.

In the faint light from the cave 'chimney', Pethi spoke to Vleppo; the cat's eyes glowed as he listened.

'Up there, see? To my mother. Zoë. You go to Zoë. Understand, Vleppo?'

The cat's eyes narrowed slightly. He understood, it seemed. He looked round at the rocky walls. Then he sprang. Once, twice, from one rock to another. Then was in the base of the chimney, outlined against the clumps of grey-lit ferns. He looked down at Pethi.

'All right. I'm coming some of the way.' It looked an impossible climb, but here with the goddess anything could be done. He glanced at her calm face and, lightfooted, made his way up the cave wall, clinging superhumanly to rough stone, finally to swing himself alongside Vleppo in the opening. The cat at once climbed on upwards.

The chimney bent craggily, one way and another. It was easier to climb than Pethi had expected, although some of the stones were loose, and clattered down to the cave below from under his toes. He climbed until he was out of breath: Vleppo still sprang ahead of him. Pethi sat on a broad shelf made by the chimney bending almost at a right-angle. He would rest a while before climbing back down.

'Go ahead, Vleppo,' he called. 'Take our note to Zoë.'

Vleppo's sure, large feet paused a moment: he glanced down, flicked his tail, and moved swiftly on. Yes, he'll get there, Pethi knew. He could climb on up himself, he supposed, but what was the point? He had no idea where the chimney emerged, but surely it would be on Thanos' land, and he had no wish to be spotted by one of those guards.

He looked round the ledge where he sat. Here several clumps of ferns grew sturdily, and one brilliant cushion of pink flowers. Pethi bent forward to pick one, to take back to Tini. As he did, his weight went on to his left hand, and a large stone moved beneath it. He felt among the ferns to pick it up, and was about to toss it to the back of the shelf without a glance when something stopped him.

He looked at the stone, and his insides twisted. It was a

sculpted hand, broken off along a diagonal line from base of thumb to middle of palm below the little finger. A left hand, with gracefully curved fingers that looked as if they should be holding something. It was dirty, but Pethi could see it was marble. And he was sure it was the goddess' hand.

He turned it over in wonder. Why was it here, on this shelf? He looked up: had the statue, then, been lowered here perhaps? Broken in the attempt to hide her . . . In that case, perhaps there were more fragments, here at this natural junction in the chimney. Suddenly he remembered Vleppo, as he had arrived at this shelf on the upward climb. He had stopped, and sat down exactly where Pethi was sitting now, and yowled. It had been a hollow sound, echoed by the rocks: at the time, Pethi had taken it to mean the cat wanted him to hurry. But now . . . ? All along, Vleppo had seemed to know and understand more than he and Tini. Had accepted the mysteries of the goddess' cave calmly. And Pethi could not forget that it was the kitten Vleppo who had first brought him here.

He began to feel about him on the rocky shelf, lifting plants and ferns, investigating every loose-feeling stone. But he found nothing more. Until, giving up, ready to descend to the cave again, he shifted from where he sat. And something moved beneath him. Something large.

He edged round the shelf, and began to tear at the growth of weeds and lumps of rock. Gradually, it emerged. Covered in dirt and small stones, overgrown with thick rock-plant, it took Pethi at least ten minutes to uncover only half. But he could see now that the thing he had been sitting on . . . the thing Vleppo had briefly stopped at . . . was a huge shield.

It was a shield intricately carved and decorated, circular.

The material, he thought, might be ivory, and the decorations were in some metal, blackened by age. Gold, perhaps? And in the centre of the shield, exquisitely worked, the wonderfully grotesque face of the Medusa, with her hair of snakes twining and writhing. It could only be the shield of the goddess Athene.

* * *

Tini turned over the heavy marble hand, and listened to Pethi's gabbled story.

'Shield, and snakes . . .' she said. 'Pethi – that tape-recording, if anyone can understand it. It *must* tell something.' She glanced out of the cave mouth. 'If we ever get out of here.'

'We will.' Pethi was certain. 'And Tini – Vleppo. He seemed to know the shield was there. He stopped, and miaowed at me in a peculiar way.'

'Somehow,' Tini said, 'that doesn't surprise me.'

'He'll get there, all right. All we do now is wait.' Pethi flopped. 'Anything happened out there?'

'The guard changed. Thanos must have a fair army on the island,' Tini said cynically. 'Maybe that was why he was so pleased with himself this morning.'

Pethi peered out. 'Maybe. He's certainly being careful. I can see five men now.'

'Five!'

'I dare say they're all over the clifftops. They seem to be talking together. Oh, they're eating. I can see one of them with a bottle. Beer I suppose.'

'Lunchtime. I'm starving.'

They chewed on what was left of the bread and cheese and sipped some lemonade, saving the rest.

The day lasted for ever. They took turns to sleep and watch. The men on the cliff stayed, mopping their heads as the sun filled the afternoon sky, grouping, talking. Thanos came twice, staying only a few minutes.

'Vleppo should be back by now.' The sun was lower. Pethi glanced towards the back of the cave. 'Maybe I should go down and wait for him there.'

'He'll be all right. Maybe he'll wait for dark too.'

Earlier Pethi had felt confident. Now, as the afternoon went on, anxiety grew. What if Vleppo had been seen? Or his mother hadn't been around? If Dimitrios didn't get back as well? Every time Pethi glimpsed the cheerful Thanos at the clifftop he became more worried.

The sun was at last sinking, 'reigning in the sky', as the islanders said. The whole world was burning, glorious.

'Don't you want some sleep?' Pethi asked.

'I'm not tired now.' Tension kept their senses alive. Tini peered out of the cave. 'They don't seem to be doing anything. There's Thanos again. There are even more men. In a group, talking. Oh! Oh, god!'

'What?'

'Vleppo. I can see Vleppo. It must be.'

Pethi shoved her aside. '*Where?*'

'Top of the cliff. Where we started down.'

It was true. Small, at that distance, but definitely Vleppo. He slunk low, a black shape, making for the place where the descent began. The men were facing in the other direction.

'Holy mother of god. Why is he coming back that way?'

Pethi's eyes were pinned on the group of men as the cat crept along, only metres from them. If none of them turned round . . . if they stayed like that, in an inward facing group . . . yes, Vleppo was going to make it. Surely. Slowly, the cat crept, as if hunting, close to the ground. Pethi didn't breathe. Tini watched his face.

Vleppo was directly above the first ledge down. With a sleek movement, he stood, and was over.

'He's there. He's there. No!' Pethi swore in anguish. 'They saw him. They saw.'

'Oh no.'

One of the men had turned in the last second, and seen the cat's tail and hind legs slip over the cliff edge. Pethi watched him point, as if disbelieving. Some of the other men laughed: they thought he had been seeing things. But Thanos didn't laugh. He led the man to the edge, asking him to show the place he had seen the cat. Now they were both peering down the cliff.

'What's happening?' Tini whispered.

'They're looking down the cliff.' Pethi's voice was desperate. 'They can see him.'

The man with Thanos raised his rifle to his shoulder, laughing, and aimed down the cliff at Vleppo. Pethi leapt to his feet. But even as he felt he must hurl himself from the cave, Thanos pushed the man's gun aside. The shot split the evening at the same moment. Tini gasped, almost screamed. Pethi sat down, shaking.

'It's all right,' he managed. 'The man missed. Thanos made him miss.'

'*Thanos* did?'

Pethi's voice was weary. 'Now Thanos knows I'm about here somewhere. He'll watch where Vleppo goes.'

'He won't follow?'

'He might. He's quite agile. Or send some of the men.'

Tini was quavering with fear. 'But they'd be afraid. They might fall.'

'Don't forget Thanos knows there must be a way down that cliff. I brought back the kitten. And if he's determined . . . '

'Why should he be? Why bother with you?'

'I'm in his way. Like Dimitrios. That's all, I suppose.'

'I'll watch for a bit.' She pulled Pethi back from the entrance. He had had enough for the moment.

'Vleppo's making his way down.' She watched the lithe movements of the cat in the pink glow of the sun. 'He's almost under the bulging part. They won't be able to see him soon. Thanos is kneeling at the top, looking over. All the other men have turned up – there must be ten or twelve of them. Thanos has stood up. He's arguing. Nobody wants to follow. Thanos is pointing at the sun. He must be saying it'll be dark soon. He seems to be angry. Oh.'

'Oh what?'

'He's started himself.'

Pethi had to look. Thanos was standing on the first ledge down. Two of the men, one with a rifle, were being told to follow. They were reluctant, but Thanos no doubt had the power. And the money.

'Holy mother.'

'I can't watch. I feel sick.'

'Why did Vleppo come back that way?' Pethi asked again.

'He's not stupid. There must be a reason.'

Slowly the men followed Vleppo's route.

'We could hide in the goddess' cave,' Tini said.

'I'm not moving from here until Vleppo arrives.'

'No. Of course not. Nor am I.'

'You could,' Pethi realized. 'You could hide, and I'll wait. Then at least you'd be sure of getting away. They probably don't know you're here as well.'

'You must be mad,' Tini dismissed it.

Thanos was following the ledges accurately and carefully. Vleppo was now almost at the big platform, proceeding leisurely. Pethi waited for him to spring from one side to the other: soon after that, the cat would be out of sight from the cave.

Tini watched Pethi's face. 'What's happened?' she cried, as he gasped.

'He's stopped. Vleppo stopped. He – for god's sake, he's sitting there, washing himself. Anyone'd think he wanted them to catch up.' Pethi's aghast face turned to Tini. She shook her head in incomprehension: her heart was moving too fast to answer.

When Pethi looked back towards the cliffs, Vleppo was out of sight. He had jumped across the chasm and must now be making his way along the ledge to the cave. Thanos and his men were almost at the platforms.

High on the opposite cliff, the rest of Thanos' men watched and waited. They talked together, shrugging and gesturing: evidently it was beyond understanding, Thanos' preoccupation with this black cat.

'They're at the platform.' Pethi saw the three figures standing together. 'They can't get lost now.'

Despairing, they sat in the cave. They could only wait for Vleppo to spring into the entrance, and for Thanos to arrive a few paces behind. With men, and guns.

'Listen,' Pethi said urgently. 'We'll move to the back of this cave, just to where the slope begins. We'll lie down, and wait. Then we'll see Vleppo appear at the mouth of the cave, and he's bound to come straight towards me. As soon as he does, we'll go down to the goddess' cave. We can hide in the chimney. They won't find us there.'

'All right.' There was nothing else.

They crawled to the back of the dark cave and waited, eyes fixed open on the now twilit sky. Pethi wondered if Tini could hear the fantastic din his heart seemed to be making. They dared not speak. They hardly dared draw breath.

A man's voice cutting through the silence made them jump. 'It's going to that devil-ridden cave.' That wasn't Thanos. 'It's bewitched. You know that I suppose.' The man was angry and afraid; whoever he was, he knew something of the folk stories of Serifos. They heard Thanos laugh in contempt. The men were very near. Surely Vleppo must arrive soon.

And then he was there. Ears up, whiskers out, he sprang into sight, a smooth silhouette in the cave mouth. Tini heard Pethi's breath let out. 'Vleppo,' he hissed. 'Over here.'

But the expected didn't happen.

Inexplicably, horrifyingly, Vleppo walked only a few quick steps towards Pethi, and stopped. Then he turned, sat down, and gazed towards the cave mouth. The sound of the men's feet, shuffling along the ledge, was now clear. And some breathing.

'Vleppo . . . !' The appalled whisper bounced off the rocks.

The cat ignored it. He remained, a sleek watchful shape. The tip of his tail flicked swiftly up and down. Any moment now, the men must be here.

Hardly realizing they were doing so, Pethi and Tini were crawling forward towards Vleppo. It was essential to get him, to escape down the cave tunnel and hide. Quickly. Nearer they crawled with awful stealth. The cat was utterly still. Thanos could be heard clearly: 'Got that torch?'

'Vleppo,' breathed Pethi, in agony, and lifted his hands to capture the cat.

Too late. The upper half of Thanos seemed to fill the cave mouth. Tini shrank. Pethi froze.

It was a few seconds before Pethi realized that Thanos would not be able to see them. There was little or no light left now in the cave. Thanos himself was a black hulk against the pale sky. Vleppo remained a statue.

The second man came alongside, shorter than Thanos.

'Well,' Thanos' voice was softly pleased. 'You see, it wasn't so bad.'

His partner said sharply: 'I'm not going in there after some cat.'

Thanos replied with a laugh. The noise crashed about the cave. 'You'll go if I pay. Eh? And you're in no place to argue.' The man said nothing. Pethi saw him shrug as if in bravado.

'Marko – ' Thanos called, presumably to the third man. 'I'll have the torch . . . ' He reached out an arm. The second man was taking his rifle off his back. In the cave, nobody breathed.

Thanos' hand returned, holding a large flashlight torch. Pethi and Tini watched as he peered at it, looking for the switch.

The next thing that happened they would never completely lose from their minds.

As the white torch beam leapt out, Vleppo acted. Afterwards Pethi realized how terrifying a sight he must have been to the men. Even from inside the cave, seen against the light, he was shock enough. Their hearts jumped savagely.

Vleppo sprang forward to within a handspan of Thanos, with a scream that was echoed and re-echoed chillingly in the cave. Then a long, curdling yowl, a snarl, and spitting. His fur stood out, making him twice his size. His eyes were enormous, brilliant in the light. His teeth gleamed long and white. Sharp claws were ready.

For Thanos there was a half-second of fixed horror. Then he reeled backwards, off balance. The man with him gave a shriek of terror at this grotesque cave-devil. The torch left Thanos' hand, flying in an arc against the sky. His arms flailed.

'He'll fall!' Tini screamed. The noise was nothing amid Vleppo's snarls and the men's shouts of fear. Thanos clutched in desperation at the cave edge. At once Vleppo's big paw struck out, sinking claws. Thanos' scream was of pure terror. He snatched back his hand, losing balance again, lurching back and forth in suspended time. Pethi and Tini could not move. Thanos grabbed at the man beside him, who was standing transfixed, unable to use his gun, staring bulge-eyed into the dark cave. But Thanos threw him off balance now: the man panicked, shrieking at him to let go, trying to shake him off.

Thanos did let go. With a wild effort, he threw himself sideways to clutch at the rocky cliff face. He wanted nothing but to escape the cave. He gave no thought to the man standing next to him. And with such force did Thanos move, he knocked his partner right off the ledge.

The scream seemed to go on for minutes.

When Pethi raised his head, Thanos was utterly motionless in the cave mouth, clinging to the side. Petrified. Vleppo too was still: a rigid, muscular, softly-snarling threat.

Then, tremblingly careful, Thanos edged away, back along the ledge. Pethi stared numbly at the empty section of sky, hearing Thanos' feet shuffle, and stop.

Thanos' voice came back, shaking with hatred and fear, sharp with hysteria: 'Now you can stay there and starve, boy. Come out, and we'll pick you off the cliff.' Pethi said nothing. Again he heard Thanos' feet move, and then a muttered voice. The third man, Marko, shouted now, strained and angry:

'Yes. You wait there. For ever. Like his brother!' The words clattered horribly in the cave.

It was some moments before Pethi could move forward to join Vleppo. The cat was sitting on the extreme edge of the cave entrance, looking upwards. Pethi followed his stare to the top of the facing cliff. Thanos' men were standing blackly against the last pearl light in the sky; as Tini had said, about a dozen of them. In a curving line they stood, the guns in their hands held down. They were as still as stone.

IO

Tini was still lying face down on the cave floor.

'There was a note on Vleppo,' Pethi said softly. 'The boat will be here soon.'

'That man,' she said, muffled. 'He'll be dead.'

There was a silence.

'We'd be dead by now,' Pethi finally said. 'If Vleppo hadn't defended us.'

There was too much to say, so they said nothing. Tini sat up slowly.

'It's dark. Are the men still there?'

'I don't know.' Pethi gave her the last of the lemonade. 'There are no lights.'

'Dimitrios.' Tini still sounded stunned. 'Thanos has stopped him somehow.'

'I think so.' Pethi tried to sound calm, but he feared for his friend.

Tini reached out in the dark and held Pethi's hand.

'We'll have to go down.'

'Yes. If you feel all right.'

The moon would soon rise, but tonight thick clouds were forming mounds across the sky: with every second the darkness grew.

'I'll risk the torch,' Pethi said.

'What if they shoot?' Her voice shook, 'Pick us off, like he said.'

'It's a small light, I don't see how they could hit us, especially as we'll be moving further away from them. And I won't keep it on all the time. Anyway, I'm not so sure many of those men will have wanted to stay on guard.' He paused. 'The ledge is quite wide, so even though we don't know it, it shouldn't be too bad. But I think it'd be too dangerous with no light at all.'

'I'm ready.' Tini was numbed, feeling nothing.

Pethi slung the duffel-bag over his shoulders, then took Tini's hand. 'The *Petros* must be waiting,' he said gently. 'It'll be all right.' He pushed out of his mind the scream of the falling man, the sheer cliff; the *Petros* would take them away from here. They must find out about Dimitrios.

Vleppo led the way. Pethi flicked the torch light ahead briefly, and then off. He moved a few steps, and helped Tini to join him. They edged along to the first corner with painful slowness, every nerve waiting for the sound of a rifle shot. But there was silence.

Round the corner they felt safer, and the ledge broadened at once. Still, not knowing what to expect, they moved like snails. It was dark. The rocks shone only briefly under the torch light. A few steps were taken, a stop. Tini's jaw was rigid with fear: she found herself imagining that man falling, falling. She clung to the rocks in terror. The world was black.

'I can't move.'

'Yes, you can.' Pethi's heart battered. She was an arm's length away. 'Yes you damn well can,' he almost shouted.

She was stuck, trembling. 'I can't, I can't.'

136

'Tini!' He was helpless. Then: 'Think of the goddess.' He didn't know what else to say.

For one endless minute, Tini was still, but then she edged towards Pethi. The goddess. They must reach the bay safely. She must not think of the hideous plunging distance beneath her.

Slowly, silently, down. With each tiny step that took them further from Thanos and nearer the sea, they felt easier.

'We must be more than half-way,' Pethi said once. 'Now the ledge will get really wide, I remember. It'll be fine.' It was.

And at last they stood on the flat rocks of the cliff base. Staring into the night. Water lapped, sheltered from the wind. Nothing could be seen. Pethi waved his torch in circles, briefly.

At once, George's voice: 'Pethi. Tini. Here,' it said firmly, comforting beyond description. He waited in a small rowing boat just ahead of them, by high rocks. Pethi picked up Vleppo, clasped Tini's hand, and flew towards him.

'Is it all right to light a lamp?' George was a silhouette, helping them into the dinghy.

'Dad!' Tini sank into his solid arm.

'Men on the cliff, we think,' Pethi answered him. George grunted, and without asking questions began to row strongly away from the rocks. In minutes the *Petros* was swaying darkly beside them.

There was a confused business of being pulled on board, when limbs seemed to lose all strength, of George tying up the dinghy as Zoë hugged Pethi and Tini and thrust them on to bunks in a dimly-lit cabin. Warm air, trapped here from the sunny day, sank into their exhausted skins.

'Say nothing,' Zoë ordered, confronting them with bowls of soup, steaming a welcome. George clambered down into the cabin.

'Well,' he said to his daughter, sitting beside her, 'you certainly scared the living daylights out of me.'

Zoë saw the tears begin to pour down Tini's face and into her soup before George did.

'What a fool you are!' she cried in English. 'She is exhausted – '

George was amazed at Zoë and ashamed. 'Sorry, sorry,' he muttered, his arms round Tini. Now she couldn't stop the tears.

'It's all right,' she wobbled, 'I'm worn out, and there's a man dead, and the goddess. And Thanos . . . ' she managed to control herself, gulping.

'Have your soup,' Zoë said kindly, pushing George away.

'I'll tell you it all,' Pethi said tiredly, 'but first – Dimitrios.'

Zoë and George looked at each other.

Pethi saw. 'He hasn't come back, has he?'

George shook his head. 'No. We've been trying to find out what happened. I'd suggested to him last night he make a phone call to the post office once he was in Athens – leaving some message for me, not using his name – to let us know he'd arrived. But nothing came.'

Pethi was afraid. 'I knew it. Thanos laughing, and he said . . . oh, never mind. So what did you find out?'

'Eat that soup,' instructed Zoë. Pethi obeyed.

'I spoke to Pavlos, his fisherman friend. He wasn't going to tell a thing, but Aspassia explained, and he could see how worried she was. He said Dimitrios had set off for Piraeus, alone, once they were all outside the harbour.'

'So Thanos couldn't have suspected anything?'

'No. But later in the night Pavlos went to Kythnos, to deliver something to a relative I think. He spoke to some fishing friends there, and one of them told him he'd seen Dimitrios' caique earlier, east of Kythnos.'

'There's nothing odd about that. He'd go that way to Piraeus.'

George shook his head, worried. 'Wait. The point is this. Pavlos' friend was in a little boat, and Dimitrios' caique passed him quite near. He could hear Dimitrios singing, for quite a time after the boat had gone. Then, it stopped. Suddenly, I mean. And the engine too. He thought he heard some shouting. And the next thing was, he heard the engine again, getting louder. Dimitrios' caique came back. He said it passed quite close again, only this time it was headed east, to cut across the north tip of Kythnos, steering he thought for Syros. And Dimitrios wasn't singing any more.'

Pethi stared at George's and Zoë's faces. At first he thought: why would Dimitrios suddenly head for Syros? And then . . .

'That damned Thanos,' Zoë angrily explained. 'Nobody thought of that.'

'Somebody already on the boat.' Pethi's voice was flat. Then he leapt up. 'What's the point in waiting, then?' he cried. He pulled open a drawer in the table, dragging out charts. 'Syros . . . it won't take us all that long.'

He was out of the cabin and starting the engine. He didn't care if any of Thanos' men on the cliff heard the sound. The engine would be quicker than sail. All that mattered was getting to the island of Syros, finding out if Dimitrios had been seen there. If anyone knew anything at all. Fear filled Pethi, as he remembered Thanos' menacing words.

Zoë came out of the cabin and watched him for a moment. Then she said: 'It's a fair way to Syros. George and I will look after the boat while you sleep.'

He shook his head.

'Yes,' she said firmly. 'I can handle the boat as well as you can. Nothing else can be done until we get there.'

He gave in. The thought of the soft bunk almost made his bones melt.

In the cabin George was standing looking at Tini, already sleeping, affection and thoughtfulness on his face. Pethi, before he collapsed on to the other bunk, plunged into the duffel-bag, and brought out the sculpted marble hand, the hand of the goddess.

'Take a look at that, George,' he said, and flopped, with Vleppo beside him. At once, it seemed, he was asleep, the vibration of the *Petros*' engine a wonderful comfort.

George was left speechlessly turning over the hand, his questions cruelly forced to wait.

*   *   *

Sometime after midnight Pethi awoke. The engine had stopped, and the movement told him they were anchored, or moored. He was off his bunk and out of the cabin in one swooping motion.

'Just arrived.' Zoë met him. 'Syros.'

Pethi had never been to this busy port before: all around him ships were at anchor. On shore, the harbour lights were bright.

'It's big,' George said.

'I know the name of the taverna Dimitrios goes to here,' Pethi remembered. 'Yorgos. That's it.'

Rapidly he and George, Vleppo right behind them, untied the dinghy and began to row for the nearest jetty. The moon was up, but there was none of the astounding brilliance of the previous night. Dark, fluff-edged clouds crowded across the sky; the water was oily black.

A fisherman greeted them curiously at the jetty, and Pethi asked him the way to Yorgos' taverna. It wasn't far.

It was a big room, of cigarette smoke and voices under bare electric bulbs. Syros, it seemed, stayed awake all night. Card games were being played, men ate and drank. Stories were being told, arguments enjoyed.

Yorgos himself, the tired-looking owner, told them it had been a full week since he had seen Dimitrios there. He shrugged, dismissingly, looking with curiosity at the shock-haired boy and his cat, and the worried foreigner in spectacles. Men at the tables stared, shook heads, shrugged. 'Dimitrios?' they said, answering Pethi and George, '*Ochi*. No. Why are you looking for him?' To be disturbed at the absence of a fisherman was eccentric: often they were gone from home for weeks to do their work. But there was no time to explain. Were there other tavernas that Dimitrios might visit? Yes, one or two, they said leisurely. Yorgos told them the names, while insisting that Dimitrios would never visit Syros and not eat here, with him.

Pethi strode out, Vleppo and George at his heels. He felt hopeless. Still, they must try.

They asked at the places whose names they'd been given. They went to several others as well. Not one person had seen Dimitrios. It was a waste of time.

Despairingly they returned to the jetty.

'What can we do?' Pethi asked George. He refused to think of what Thanos might have arranged for Dimitrios. He would not believe that he might never see his friend again.

'Is there any other island the caique might have been making for? Beyond Syros?' George asked.

Pethi looked at him. 'Any number,' he was dejected. 'Tinos, Mykonos, Andros – just think of a name. For all I know it could have kept going until the Turkish coast.'

They stood on the jetty looking down at the dinghy, strangely reluctant to leave Syros where they had come in hope.

'Come on,' George said eventually, a hand on Pethi's shoulder.

At that moment running feet at the beginning of the jetty made the timbers bounce and creak. A voice called:

'Eh! Eh!'

Pethi spun. A fisherman gasped up to them.

'You wanted Dimitrios, eh?'

'Yes, yes!' Pethi nearly seized him. 'You've seen him?'

The man leaned on the jetty rail, getting his breath, waving a burned brown hand north-west.

'His boat, the blue caique with the white stripe, I saw her at dawn . . . '

'Where?' George and Pethi shouted together.

'Ghíaros.'

'*Ghíaros*?' It was a tiny, bare rock of an island, the nearest to Syros.

'I thought it strange. Yes, very strange.' The fisherman was breathing more slowly now, relaxing, becoming maddeningly conversational. 'I've never known Dimitrios go there. But I saw it, oh definitely, the caique. In a little cove on the north side. Quite deserted. I thought to myself – ah, yes, it is certainly Dimitrios' caique, but where is Dimitrios? Having a rest perhaps, asleep in his cabin. Or perhaps the men have all gone ashore. I couldn't see a soul. It was odd, very odd. And – '

'Thank you, thank you – ' Pethi was into the dinghy, Vleppo springing after. 'Come on George.'

'My name's Yiannis,' the man said to George. 'Dimitrios is an old friend. He and I – '

George shook Yiannis' hand. 'Thank you,' he said, and got quickly into the dinghy.

The keen brown face watched from the jetty. Yiannis wanted to talk on, but had to content himself with a hasty, grateful wave from Pethi and a shouted promise to return and explain. He stood, smiling, as the little boat made for the *Petros*. It was good enough: hospitality had been given to the stranger.

Hope was almost swamped by fear as the *Petros* moved out of the port. Dimitrios' caique deserted, rocking in a lonely cove he never visited. It was the luck of the gods that anyone had seen it at all, let alone anyone who would know the boat. Still ... Pethi thought ... it had been seen. The luck of the gods ... ? Perhaps it was with them still. He thought of the marble hand, the hand of the goddess.

He looked at George, who was bending over one of the sea charts, studying the coastline of the little island of Ghíaros. George must be seething with questions about the sculpture and the cave, but had kept silent, helping him search for Dimitrios. Pethi had liked George from the day they had met, but now, with sudden clarity, he saw George's silence as a sign of friendship unusually solid.

'George,' he said, when they had discussed the best course. 'The hand.'

'Coffee,' said Zoë, appearing at the hatchway with Tini right behind her carrying hunks of buttered bread. 'We thought we'd need breakfast at regular intervals.' She distributed hot cupfuls, and stared at the chart with George. 'Ghíaros. God. It's no more than an awful rock.'

'He might be all right . . . mightn't he?' Tini asked feebly. It was unbearable that anything had happened to Dimitrios.

'Of course.' Pethi nodded. And at once began to ask George about the north coast of the island, and how they would begin to explore the coves there. George showed him the map.

'We'll have to wait for dawn,' Pethi said. 'It's rocky. And we'd better use sail, not the engine. Just in case anyone's still about that we don't want to meet . . . '

Everyone crammed into the small seating space near the wheel, silently gnawing bread and drinking coffee. Pethi felt wide awake. His sleep had been deep, and now all his concentration was on steering his boat the quickest way towards Ghíaros. Tini, too, was refreshed. The cave seemed days away. Except . . .

'Did you look at the hand?' she asked her father.

'We were about to talk just as breakfast arrived,' he smiled. She could see his eyes shining in the lamplight. 'Pethi had just begun.'

It seemed the time to tell it all, as they cut through the sea, leaving the coast of Syros behind.

'What did you think of it?' Pethi wanted to know.

George breathed deeply. 'Well,' he said, and his voice

trembled a little. 'I can hardly believe it, but – yes. It's classical.'

Pethi smiled. 'And?'

'It's very white marble – perhaps from Paros? And part of quite a large statue. A hand that was holding something – but a woman's hand I think.'

Pethi and Tini beamed at him.

Zoë lost patience. 'You two!' she cried. 'Tell it – come on, what is it?'

'All right,' Pethi agreed. 'You're right, George, it is part of a statue. Of a woman. In fact,' he paused, looking briefly at Tini, but she was watching her father's face, 'we believe it's a statue of the goddess Athene.' George gasped. Pethi went on: 'Her head is in the cave.'

George couldn't speak.

Tini said: 'We have a kind of proof that it's Athene, though it's not proof that many people would believe. Or understand.'

'Proof?' George managed at last.

'Here,' said Zoë, pushing Pethi away from the wheel. 'I'll take over while you talk.'

They told it right from the beginning, when Pethi first followed Vleppo to the cave. Zoë made outraged noises at learning of the dangers her son had been in, but otherwise said little. George became more and more excited, finding paper and pencil, making Pethi do sketches of the goddess' helmet, then staring at them in wonder and amazement. 'Oh, it's not possible,' he kept whispering in English. '*Incred*ible.'

Describing the feeling the cave gave Pethi was not easy, and when they came to the part of the mysterious voice, Tini

145

speaking words that came from somewhere out of her control, George was first sceptical, then silent and anxious. At the end, he said blankly:

'But you don't know any ancient Greek.'

'No. I don't.'

Pethi said: 'You'd understand it, wouldn't you, George, if you heard it? You could translate?'

George nodded, still gazing at Tini in a vaguely worried way. 'I imagine so. I can speak it and write it.'

'Well that's why we went back to the cave last night, to record the words.'

They explained how they had decided to tell of their secret, Pethi making apologetic noises about his initial anger at George's first mention of archaeology on Serifos.

'I wasn't going to tell Tini,' Pethi said. 'But it just happened.'

Tini explained their fear that the mystery might go for ever if the goddess were taken from the cave. They had to try again before Thanos' men were on guard.

Zoë exploded here. 'Dear mother of god!' she accused her son. 'You took Tini to that cave in the dark! I have just realized. Are you mad? Mad?'

'There was a moon,' Pethi said. 'Watch the course.'

'Bah!' she replied, and attended to the steering.

George was waiting. 'And you recorded the words?' he hardly dared to hope.

'Yes. Tassos lent us a tape recorder. Tini spoke for about a quarter of an hour, I think.'

George stared at Tini again. This was beyond belief.

'And you've got it? On tape? A quarter of an hour of ancient Greek?' He was almost gabbling.

146

Zoë was strangely unsurprised in her timeless Greek way; she accepted the mysteriousness of the story without attempt to analyse. She said once to Tini: 'Your name. Isn't it really Athene? I think George said so.' And nodded, as if the whole thing made sense.

Pethi was quoting the classical words he had recognized. George was nodding excitedly, though still unable to look at Tini without anxiety.

'Are you sure you're all right?' he asked her. 'No after-effects?' He wasn't sure what he expected.

'Of course I'm all right.' She became impatient with him. 'Worse things than that happened.'

They finished the story, from Thanos' men arriving at dawn. George couldn't sit still when Pethi began to describe the find in the cave chimney; more sketches, of the intricate shield, had to be made. Then the terrifying events of the evening. The man, knocked to his death by Thanos' fear of Vleppo. Their own slow descent in the dark.

'Dear god,' said George, an arm round his daughter. Zoë said nothing.

Pethi took over the wheel again. 'When all this is over,' he said, 'we'll play the tape.' The story told, ending with their own escape from the unscrupulous Thanos, Dimitrios was in all their minds again. And Aspassia. 'Poor Aspassia, just waiting,' Zoë said.

The *Petros* kept straight for Ghíaros.

II

Jason's reddish lashes gleamed above feathery shadows as Aspassia held up the lamp. He slept still. That much was good. Aspassia sighed, carrying the light back to George's kitchen table, putting it down in a tangle of knitting. She had walked through the house more than knitted that night. Waiting. Looking out at the frayed clouds. She never even thought of sleep. Only of Pavlos' story about Dimitrios' caique. And of Thanos.

Her face was expressionless with fatigue as she looked out of the window at the hint of light behind the mountain. Dimitrios should have been home by sunset yesterday, and here was dawn.

'They will surely find him,' Pavlos had comforted her last night when he brought news that he had seen the *Petros* leave the island: so Pethi and Tini were safe. Aspassia had said nothing, her brown hands clasped tightly in her lap. She felt no hope; only a deep dread of what Thanos might have done. And now, another day. Where was the *Petros* now? Where her husband?

When the knock came at the door it was so slight that Aspassia thought it imagination. But again, louder. Opening the door, she was silent in disbelief. The woman Damia stood in the grey light, a woollen shawl over her head, her eyes wide and afraid. Behind her, a young girl, her maid.

'*Kyría* . . . ' Damia whispered the formal address.

Aspassia said nothing, but walked back into the house. Damia hovered, then followed. Her maid cowered behind. They stood, fearful, waiting for Aspassia to speak. But the older woman turned only to stare coldly, her hostility for Thanos directed at anything that was his.

'Forgive me,' Damia still whispered. 'I could come to nobody else. I am afraid.' Her eyes appealed. 'I am afraid. It is Thanos – '

'It is Thanos!' Aspassia's voice crackled. 'It is always Thanos if there is anything bad.' She seemed to loom over the shivering Damia. 'Have you heard, then, the wicked things he has done? Where is my husband Dimitrios, your Thanos' own brother? Is that what you have heard?' She looked as if she might seize and shake her visitor. The little servant began to weep as Damia shrank back.

'Dimitrios? I don't know. I don't know.'

Aspassia saw it was true. She looked at Damia's pale face, so young, so foolish, and sighed. Poor child. To be cursed with loving Thanos. She turned to the stove and clattered coffee pots.

'So? What is Thanos doing that brings you here?'

The words came gabbling. 'Nothing. That is, he is mad I think. Sick. I am afraid. I don't know what to do. He will kill me if I get the doctor. I couldn't think what – and then, you – you're family – '

'Ha!' Aspassia stirred coffee viciously.

' – he has been sitting all the night long, staring at the wall.

149

Staring only. As if he is granite. He sits there, still, his eyes white and shining, as if he sees something horrible. Something to freeze his blood. I spoke to him but he did not move, did not hear me. Even when I was on my knees, pleading, crying ... I am afraid, afraid.' Damia was weeping now. 'There are men in the house. They sit in the rooms, talking, whispering together. Or saying nothing. There is great fear. Something terrible.'

Aspassia gave her coffee, beckoning the sniffing child to the table also. 'What happened yesterday?'

'I don't know.' Damia shudderingly drank the coffee. 'Truly I don't!' she cried at Aspassia's contemptuous face. 'I was told to say nothing, but there is nothing to tell. There were men who had arrived at night-times. I heard little they said. Only something of the mines, and talk of money. I understood none of it. Yesterday afternoon they were all out of the house. I don't know where. Thanos too, most of the time. Then it was dark, and they all returned. Some were angry. Some looked afraid. Quarrelling, saying no, they would not guard. Thanos was white, saying nothing. I thought he too was angry, and I kept away. Then later I came to bring him food and found him alone, sitting. Sitting. With this terrible face – '

Aspassia said grimly: 'And what can I do?'

'Come with me. To the house. Speak to him. Please! He might hear you.'

'Hear *me*? Bah!'

'Please. I am afraid.'

Aspassia swirled her coffee cup. She was afraid herself. What had Thanos done? Something so terrible that even he could not face it, so had fallen into madness? Dimitrios? Or was it to do with the cave, the cave that old, old islanders always said was bewitched? Such stories often held truth.

'I am looking after *Kyrios* George's boy,' she said dismissingly.

Damia nodded at her maid. 'She will stay. She is good.'

Recovered from her fear, the girl nodded. She looked sturdy and capable enough. Aspassia agreed, rapidly giving her instructions, picking up a shawl. 'Come then,' she rapped at Damia, a hand on the door.

The sky was luminous, crowded with black clouds, as the two women pushed open the iron gates of Thanos' courtyard.

'Over here.' Damia crept across the stones, Aspassia followed firmly. Under an arched walk, through glass doors, across a shiny tiled floor to a thick wooden door. Aspassia knew the house: this was Thanos' small office.

'In there?' she asked, refusing to whisper. Damia drew back, nodding. Aspassia stepped forward and turned the handle.

Only one small window lit the room dimly. But quickly she saw Thanos. He sat on a hard chair, his back to the door, facing a blank wall. A rifle on the floor leaned against his chair. Thanos did not turn as the door opened and Aspassia entered. Not a finger moved. He must be asleep.

Seeing him, Aspassia was driven forward by hatred.

'Thanos!' she said loudly, striding to face him. Then stopped. Thanos was not sleeping. He sat with his eyes wide open. But although Aspassia had walked into his line of vision, there was no flicker. He might almost be dead. His face was pale, greenish. Deep grooves of black curved under his eyes. His normally smooth cheeks were haggard and stubbly. Aspassia stepped back.

'Thanos!' again, but less certain. Then she bent, grasped his arm. 'Thanos!' she shook him. 'Wake up, fool.' She neither feared nor pitied him.

His arm was as rigid as rock. There was no sign he had heard or felt her. Aspassia looked at his waxy features and thought again of the bewitched cave; a superstitious fear made her hesitate. Then she remembered her husband. Now she shouted directly in Thanos' face. 'Thanos! Where is Dimitrios? Where? Your brother? My husband? Tell me, may you be cursed!' But Thanos remained impossibly still.

'All night like this,' Damia whispered at the door, weeping again. 'What shall I do? What shall I do?'

Aspassia was half aware, as Damia spoke, of a dark-coloured cat, one of the many around the house, slipping in at the open door, curiously exploring the day's beginning. The cat reached her feet, sniffed idly at her shoes. Then, with a low yowl, it sprang on to the motionless knee of Thanos.

Afterwards Aspassia knew she had shouted and flung herself down behind a table, and Damia screamed, high and piercing.

As the cat landed softly on Thanos, the room erupted. Thanos came out of his stillness with a hideous, inhuman, terrified roar, flying to his feet. The cat part-fell, part-jumped away from him . . . but not to escape. Thanos caught up his rifle. Twice the gun exploded crashingly in the small room: it was as if the walls had shattered. Aspassia, crouching, saw the cat on its side near the corner, as if suddenly asleep. Blood was on the floor. And Thanos stood white-faced, shouting, not real words, roaring. 'Mother of God, he is truly mad,' Aspassia muttered in terror, waiting for him to turn and discover her.

Trembling, she began to stand, hoping to run. But Thanos moved first. Staring-eyed he lumbered straight past her, knocking Damia to the floor, careering on and out into the courtyard. Yelling, yelling. Then more shots. And more. Choking, Aspassia lurched instinctively after him. Thanos must not get out into the village, that was all.

He was not in the courtyard, but the pathetic bodies of two cats lay on the pavings. Another shot – from the side of the house. Aspassia ran, gasping, through the arched walk, sickened to pass another sprawled cat on the way. She burst into the garden to see Thanos aim and kill another. He missed a second, which leapt away over the walls, spitting in terror. Thanos cursed murderously, shooting crazily after it. Then he turned, rifle ready, casting about for more. He saw Aspassia. She was too revolted to be afraid.

'You are mad, Thanos!' she screamed at him. 'At last, you are mad.' Wildly, though shaking and exhausted, she ran towards him as if somehow she could stop what he was doing. But he hurled her aside and strode back to the house. She stumbled, nearly fell. When she had got her breath, she ran after him.

In the courtyard he was handing his gun to one of the men who had emerged in alarm at the shots. They were all strangers to Aspassia. 'Now,' Thanos was saying in a thick, angry voice. 'At once. And finish him for sure.'

The man had hurried out of the gates before Aspassia realized what the words meant. And then she flew at Thanos with her nails and all her strength, in fury and horror, screaming to know where Dimitrios was. Thanos struck out at her: two men seized her as Thanos walked into the house, held her as she tried desperately to go after the man with the rifle.

When they let her go, the white launch was moving fast away from the jetty, to head for Ghíaros.

12

They came slinking along the coast of the peaked rock that was Ghíaros. Silently, with sails curving before the breeze.

It was in the third or fourth cove. They crept round a craggy headland, peering into the grey light. And there she was. The blue and white caique moved gently, near the shore, as the wind stirred the clear green water. To Pethi, after so much fear and anxiety, it was unreal.

At once he brought the *Petros* into the wind, and the sails were dragged down.

Nothing, nobody else was about. Behind the caique rose the bare, reddish hillside. No house, no path. A scrubby greenness, hardly there at all, could be seen high up where the island met the pale sky. Silence.

If they spoke at all, it was in whispers. Sound carries over water, and the caique was barely fifty metres away. If one of Thanos' men was still on board, awake, he would have heard them already, and seen them too. But they prayed that any guard would be sleeping. And let him stay that way, until they reached the boat.

Zoë and Tini stayed at the wheel, in case the *Petros* had to move away fast. Vleppo stayed too, his eyes glowing calmly it seemed, at Pethi's hissed instructions.

Carefully, soundlessly, Pethi and George moved off in the

dinghy. Nearer they slid, easing round the blue hull. Now they saw that Dimitrios' caique was anchored, and a mooring rope too had been thrown round a needle of rock. The boat had been made safe.

Nothing moved. Not even a seabird cried. Silence hung over the island, and fear. George drew alongside, holding the caique at arm's length to avoid a betraying nudge. He nodded a signal to Pethi, who sprang aboard noiselessly. The boat rocked under his weight. He stood. Still no hint of a noise. Briefly he shook his head at George, and then crept towards the cabin. George waited in the dinghy, ready to row if Pethi had to make an escape.

The hatchway to the cabin was open. Pethi paused, confused for a moment. Somehow he had expected it to be closed, with the possibility of a man inside, guarding Dimitrios. The cabin being open must mean nobody was there. Someone defending the caique would have waited behind closed doors. Disappointment crept over him; no guard meant no Dimitrios.

Warily he peered into the cabin, giving his eyes time to adjust to the dimness. It was empty. No human shape. Nothing. Just a faint creaking as the boat idly rocked.

He stepped on to the rungs that would take him down into the cabin, vaguely feeling he should look around. There might be some indication of where Dimitrios was. Three rungs down, he halted, a sickening feeling lurching into his stomach. On one, of the rungs, dried blood. And again, on a lower step.

Nerves twisting, he went on down.

At the bottom of the step-ladder, he almost trod on Dimitrios, taking him for a bundle of rags.

*   *   *

156

'I think he's dead.'

Pethi's face stared shocked white from the caique. George leapt up to join him, securing the dinghy as he came.

It was only a short distance up the cabin steps, but it might have been a mountainside. Dimitrios, for a small man, was unbelievably heavy, and misery ebbed Pethi's strength almost to nothing. But at last they got him up on deck, laying him gently among the nets and ropes.

The fine-mesh net over Dimitrios' head was tied down viciously round his body at the elbows. His feet were wound round with rope. The hideous rust of dried blood caked the netting and the fisherman's rough clothes.

George said nothing as Pethi tremblingly handed him a sharp knife: he had taken it with him from his own boat, ready to use it on any attacker. Rapidly the ropes were cut. With calm, infinite care, George lifted away the fishing net, cutting through it where it stuck horribly to the man's curly hair.

Dimitrios' face was ghastly. Pethi was frozen in grief, and a creeping, frightening anger. This was his friend, with a grey, dead face. His friend and his brother all his life.

Then George said: 'He's alive.' Pethi couldn't believe.

'Pulse.' George confirmed it. 'Only just.' He stood up. 'Hospital. Athens?'

Pethi nodded, springing up before George had finished, to yell across the water to his mother to bring the *Petros* alongside. It was impossible to move fast enough. There was hope, but only a little. Pethi could see how near to death Dimitrios must be.

Then the ordeal of lifting the injured man from the caique to the *Petros*. Zoë and Tini held the two boats firmly together while it was done. 'Oh god, oh god,' Zoë was whispering to herself, over and over. And then Dimitrios was lying on one of the soft bunks, a blanket round him.

The engine roared as Pethi flung his boat about and headed away as fast as she would go from the barren cove. The blue caique rocked innocently in the wake.

'Shall I bathe his head?' Tears ran down Zoë's face.

'Better not,' George said, 'God knows what damage is done. He's barely alive.' He stared for a moment helplessly, and went on deck to help Pethi.

'Did they mean to kill him?' Tini croaked, as Zoë took and held Dimitrios' rough hand.

'I suppose not. For wouldn't they have thrown him in the sea?' Zoë was bitterly angry. 'But they've nearly killed him. And left him there, perhaps to return and get rid of him if Thanos instructed. He might die still.'

For a second Tini was back in the cave, and Thanos and his men were laughing on the clifftop at some good news. Up to now, Tini had found it hard to credit that Thanos could be as evil as she had been told; even his threatening, terrifying presence before Vleppo had saved them, had been more nightmare than truth. But now, seeing their dear Dimitrios . . .

'Where are we going?' she asked at last. She was shivering, her teeth rattling as if they were loose.

Zoë looked at her. 'Piraeus, Athens. Hospital,' she said. Then: 'Make some coffee.' Tini got up to obey.

'Isn't there any quicker way. Like a helicopter or something?'

'Yes, but we're not near enough to a route. We'd have to go to Mykonos, and that would take as long, or longer by the time it was arranged.'

On deck, George rustled charts.

'We'll stop at Kéa,' Pethi decided. 'And ask the police to telephone, have an ambulance at Piraeus.' Kéa was the next island on their route for Piraeus.

'And send a message to Aspassia, too,' George said. 'Let her know everyone's all right. Anyway, that's what we'll say. Too bad if Thanos hears about it.'

'What about Thanos? Should we tell the police at Kéa about him too?'

'Best save it for Athens. They'll deal with it, when we tell the Mining Company.'

They chugged on, not speaking. It was a grey, scudding morning. Rains hung in the skies. The wind was good, but in the wrong direction to make real speed with sail.

'He could still die.' Pethi's words were neither question nor statement.

'Yes.' George took coffee from Zoë's outstretched hand, giving some to Pethi. 'His skull must be fractured, I suppose. But perhaps it's not that bad. We can't do any more than get him to Athens.'

'Dimitrios always said he didn't care for Athens,' Pethi said irrelevantly. 'I've never been there myself,' he added.

*　　*　　*

Piraeus was a hellish dream. The ambulance waited, but so did crowds of the curious. Officials in bunches wanted to know about the *Petros*, about the unconscious man, about their names and addresses and nationalities. And the cat. What of this cat on the boy's shoulders? The police suspected conspiracy of some kind in the eccentric behaviour: was this man dead? An escaped prisoner? They began to accuse the customs officials of a blunder. Everyone shouted, bystanders joining in. One set of authorities evidently had no knowledge of what the others had arranged; there was a general feeling of having been misinformed about something important. Different uniforms railed at each other. Zoë, somewhere in the middle, shouted back at them all. They ignored her as if she were a gnat.

Pethi, white-faced as the ambulance men were bullied by George to take Dimitrios from the boat on a stretcher, said nothing. He wanted only to get his friend into Athens. But the ambulance doors were crowded about with arguing groups; some man with gold on his uniform was asking him about papers for the *Petros*. George was lost in the crowd, instructing the stretcher-bearers.

It was Tini who sorted them all out in the end, by yelling in English. George's Greek was so good he was being treated like the rest of them, questioned and harangued and pestered. But suddenly Tini was transformed into a fury, pushing her slender arms between the well-fed uniforms and thrusting the jabbering men apart. She shouted at them that Dimitrios must get to the hospital in Athens, in the ambulance, at once, or she would personally be contacting the Prime Minister, to say nothing of the British Consulate.

Whether or not they understood her didn't matter. The fact was that sufficient pause was made, from sheer astonishment, for George to help the ambulance men get Dimitrios inside and to leap in afterwards, threatening the driver with convincing punishments if he didn't drive as fast as possible to the hospital. Just before the doors closed on him, George called to Tini to follow with the others when it was all sorted out. They stared after him as the ambulance carved through the crowds towards the shrieking traffic and the road to Athens.

Dimitrios was on his way. Zoë and Tini stopped shouting; Pethi's face relaxed a little. Now he might listen to what some of these men were saying.

But the port officials looked disappointed that the centre of attraction had gone. The arguments dissipated. Policemen hung about aimlessly, trying now to look contemptuous.

After that it was comparatively simple to explain who they were and why they had arrived. They were led from one small office to another to sign papers. Pethi was convinced, and said so, that most of it was unnecessary. Curiosity was the main motive. But it did him no good: more papers were produced, more forms had to be filled.

Eventually a customs man took pity on their exhausted faces, and gave them coffee in his office. It was from him too that they borrowed a few drachmae, when they realized in alarm that George alone had money with him. With the *Petros* as guarantee of their return, they begged enough for the train fare and a little over for a taxi.

The din of Athens was astounding to Pethi. Tyres whistled on the smooth roads, brakes shrieked, drivers screamed abuse. 'I think I prefer donkeys,' he said.

'I told you cities aren't glamorous.' Tini grabbed at the side of the taxi as the driver grinningly demonstrated his cornering expertise. 'Give me Serifos any day.'

'I haven't been here since I was at school,' Zoë said. 'It's changed. But look . . . ' she pointed, ' . . . that hasn't.' The light-toned pillars of the Parthenon were luminous against the clouded sky. Pethi, seeing it for the first time, felt his heart jump. The greatest temple to Athene. Vleppo, clinging to his shoulders, also stared.

The hospital was bright, with ringing noises amid disinfected silences. They found George in a huge, echoing waiting-room. He told them the doctors were X-raying Dimitrios now.

Waiting. More waiting. They sat tired and silent, their skins tingling with salt and dust. Vaguely Pethi assessed that he ought to be hungry, but wasn't.

A doctor, clean and neat, returned to speak to George. Pethi jumped forward too. The man barely flicked a look of surprise at this scruffy, tall boy whose black hair merged into his cat's fur.

They didn't know how Dimitrios would be. Yes, his skull was fractured. Blood transfusions were essential. No, he couldn't say what the outcome would be. He was quite comfortable at the moment. Much depended on how soon he became conscious. No, it wasn't an especially severe fracture; that is to say, no pressure on the brain that needed surgery.

It was in some ways reassuring, this doctor's non-committal confidence. They had the feeling that everything was being done. George gave him some telephone numbers to call if anything should happen. The doctor calmly replied that he didn't expect anything dramatic, and recommended George to ring the hospital himself to enquire. Then, with a kindly but casual half-wave, he went.

'Well,' said George, as they all stood, looking at each other. 'We'll book into a hotel – ' seeing Tini's look, he added, 'for which Thanos will eventually pay. And bath. And have food.'

Pethi, from a great, dizzy distance, heard Tini and Zoë agree.

A good idea. Yes. But the whiteness of the hospital was daz-zlingly blurred. The room was turning over. Vleppo sprang from his shoulders a split second before Pethi collapsed on the disinfected floor.

' . . . only lack of sleep, and reaction . . . ' he heard George say placidly. 'No wonder . . . Ah. You're awake.'

Pethi stared up from the bench where he lay.

'You've only missed a minute,' Tini was assuring him. 'You looked ghastly.' She was fairly pale herself.

His mother was rubbing his hand, smiling. 'All right?'

'Yes.' He sat up. 'How peculiar. Is that fainting?'

'That's fainting,' George said cheerfully.

'Oh.' It was an indignity. But he remembered Dimitrios in the safe cool hands of the doctors, and that was all that mattered. 'I think I might be hungry,' he said.

* * *

Clean again under their battered clothes, they made for a taverna in the old part of Athens, remembered by Zoë from childhood visits. Here they gradually recovered strength under the influence of a delectable stew, *stiffádho*, and copper jugfuls of retzina wine.

They sat at a table out of doors, with the Acropolis and the Parthenon shining above them. Pethi kept looking up, his eyes dragged by the beauty of this amazing masterpiece. George saw.

'Once,' he said, 'there was a wonderful statue there, of your goddess Athene. Made by the famous sculptor Phidias, in gold and ivory. It was stolen away to Constantinople, they say. But you can see where it stood.'

Pethi nodded, as his glance crossed Tini's. They would go there before they left Athens; it didn't need to be said.

George continued to make decisions. 'We all need some sleep,' he now said, as he paid the bill.

Pethi, full of good food and feeling strangely lethargic, was happy to agree with anyone.

'And,' George went on, as they strolled back to the hotel, 'I'll be in touch with Sir Rolf, and the Mining Company.' He had already planned the rest of the stay.

They flopped into their rooms and slept.

13

It seemed later to Pethi's memory that dream was reality, and reality became dreamlike during their short stay in Athens.

Sleeping that afternoon in a cool hotel bed, he dreamt of Thanos rushing from the island in an enormous white launch, full of men with guns, while the woman Damia wept. And his goddess statue, now quite complete, was standing somewhere on a hillside. She turned into Tini, who said 'good riddance' in English. And then he was awake.

But his dream overlapped into George telling them all how, while they had slept, he'd been to see the Directors of the Mining Company, and how one of them had leapt up in anger and shouted that George was mad, it was all a wild fabrication by a foreigner, and had walked out. And how, too late, the other Directors had realized that Thanos could only have deceived the Company if he had had a senior accomplice. Police caught up on the man later, about to board a plane out of Athens, but by then it was certain he had warned Thanos by telephone. 'So I dare say he will have gone by the time the police arrive,' George regretted.

'And good riddance,' Tini said. 'As long as he never comes back to Serifos, who cares?'

'Thanos never gave up that easily,' Zoë remarked sourly.

George described how he had left the Mining Company

offices in whirling action among papers and telephones. His story merged with the unreality of them all visiting the Archaeological School, where again there were heaps and files of papers, and telephones, and people talking in excitement. And Sir Rolf Roller, speechless with amazement at the tape-recording, his teacup rattling on its saucer.

They sat in armchairs while George made frantic notes, his eyes popping in disbelief. 'Too fast!' he kept crying out in anguish. He would have to play it over many times.

It was bizarre, hearing Tini's voice from the cave here in this unfamiliar room of English furniture. Tini herself was bewildered, saying in reply to Sir Rolf's questions: 'No, I don't understand, either.' It was impossible to explain. The cave was distant, out of reach.

'Not all the words are clear,' George was saying. 'The accent is strange.'

'Of course,' Pethi remembered himself remarking as if he knew it all along, 'that will be ancient Greek the way it really was spoken, not the way you're taught it at school.'

Sir Rolf and George stared at him, and then at the little tape-recorder. Quite suddenly it was a priceless object.

'But what does it *say*?' Zoë could wait no longer.

Days later, after several playings, George discovered more detail, but that evening he could make out only a few disjointed sentences.

'About a temple that is her right,' he said, reading his notes excitedly, 'and a shield, guarded by her owl.' Tini and Pethi stared. 'And barbarians who have attacked the island. She moans, rather sadly, saying she wants to return to her temple. I think so, anyway. And something about the black crow of death making thieves, who take her treasures, fall from the cliff.' Pethi felt himself shudder. 'Treasures lie hidden – that part was quite clear – but the goddess' silver is in danger, in danger now.'

'Silver!' Pethi shot out of his chair as everything clicked into place. 'God, how stupid I am.'

'Thanos ... ' Tini was aghast. Thanos and the goddess' silver. Had he gone away, taking it?

Sir Rolf hardly glanced at their agonized faces. 'Yes, yes, any more?' He was almost tipping off his chair.

'A lot of names, place names perhaps. Maybe it's a set of directions, I can't tell. Some of it I just can't make out. And then that scream.' He looked at Tini. 'You didn't tell us.'

The shrill scream had been terrible in the shady room, startling everyone.

Tini dragged back her thoughts from the mysterious – perhaps lost – silver treasure of the goddess.

'Oh. I'd forgotten,' she said, and told about the spider and Vleppo snatching it away. 'And I'm not even afraid of spiders,' she added. Then realized that both her father and Sir Rolf were looking at her oddly. 'What?' she asked.

'Athene didn't like spiders,' George said slowly.

Sir Rolf nodded, staring at Tini, still unable to grasp and believe it all. 'True,' he murmured, 'true. Look up the myths.'

The myths. Pethi felt as if he were walking in the centre of a myth, or another dream, as he and Tini strolled over the Acropolis early next morning. The sun painted the columns of the Parthenon bright and clear. Nobody else was there. The temple soared perfectly, every line a subtle, immense beauty.

'Stop. Where you're standing.' Pethi said suddenly. 'That's where she stood. The gold and ivory statue of Athene. I read about it in the hotel last night. She was huge, much bigger than our statue. Over ten metres high.'

They wandered inside the ruined temple, walking round many times. Vleppo padded big-footed after them.

'It's peaceful here,' Tini said.

'Yes. Different from the cave, but something similar too. Maybe because we know it's Athene's.'

'It was weird – hearing the words I'd said. Wasn't it? After wondering about it so much, and then when I heard it, somehow it wasn't a surprise that it was about the temple. As if I'd half expected it. But the silver – '

'The silver! I should've realized.' Pethi blamed himself yet again. 'The goddess tried to tell me. Sending me to the boats. Thanos. I think I didn't want to believe he could know anything connected with our secret. It just had to be the mines. Whatever he's found, there must be plenty. "Riches", remember. And all those men he needed. Silver. But what? And where?'

'Near the mines somewhere. Must be.'

'The old river bed is full of pot-holes. There might even be other caves.' Pethi ran his hand over a scarred marble column. 'It must have been easy for Thanos to get someone in the Mining Company to help him close the mines, keep people out of the way. Someone who wanted to be rich too.'

'The goddess' silver treasure. Hidden somewhere near our cave . . . ' Tini spoke quietly. 'After . . . that evening, Thanos, I can't think of the cave in the same way. It's frightening now.'

'Yes. Maybe we'll never go back.'

'Maybe.'

Pethi caught hold of Tini's hand. 'D'you know what I suddenly feel is true?' She waited. 'I expect it's only my imagination, after all the tension and everything – but just then, in that moment, when we were talking about Athene, I knew that Dimitrios will be all right. Really well again.'

'I don't think it's imagination.' Tini looked down the wonderful distance of the ruined temple to where the goddess had stood over two thousand years before.

'And you were the realistic one, the believer in reason,' Pethi mocked her.

'I dare say it's realistic and reasonable,' she defended herself, 'if we only knew a bit more.' Which made Pethi laugh again. 'Even so,' she smiled, 'you know it's not imagination.'

George and Zoë, at breakfast, looked mildly surprised at them being out so early, but were full of their own news. Zoë's first words were: 'We spoke to Aspassia. The happenings on Serifos! Thanos went berserk and left. Damia is with the police – he said he'd come back for her but she doesn't believe it. They caught some men, but they don't seem to know much. But best of all –'

' – we rang the hospital again – ' said George. 'Dimitrios came round in the early hours. They say he'll be fine.'

'Yes!' Zoë's lovely face was pure joy. 'We can go and see him this morning, for a little. But he has to stay in hospital for about a month.'

Pethi and Tini smiled, as if they already knew.

From the sun-filled Parthenon to the bright little hospital

room, with Dimitrios managing a grin among the bandages when he saw Pethi.

'Eh, Pethi,' he whispered. 'They say you found me.'

Pethi wasn't able to speak.

'The *Petros*, eh? She brought me?'

Pethi nodded. Dimitrios grinned again, his gold teeth gleaming. 'How clever I was to have her ready.' His illogical smugness made Pethi grin too.

'We go back in her this morning. But we'll be visiting you. And Dimitrios – the Mining Company knows about every-thing. A chap there was in with Thanos, fixed the papers to close the mines. But it was ancient treasure Thanos'd found, we're nearly certain. Silver things. There's a lot to tell you but they said we mustn't talk to you too much.'

'They said what? Pah, doctors are mad,' Dimitrios dismissed his saviours.

'It's all good news for the island. There'll be jobs. The mines aren't finished, and there'll be a dig. And the police went to the island, but Thanos got away first – '

' – He'll be back – '

' – but I'll tell you more when we come again – '

The others came in for a few minutes, the doctor hovering behind.

Zoë took Dimitrios' hand, gently kissed his cheek.

'Ach, foolish child,' he muttered at the tears in her eyes. Then grinned at Tini. 'Hello, little angel.' He shook George's hand thanking him politely for all he had done, and then, without warning, fell asleep.

14

'Oh.' Tini stopped as soon as she stepped into the square. 'How embarrassing.'

Pethi and she had walked down the hillside to the harbour village. Unsuspecting. George and Zoë had told them to be at the square at two. Why? Nobody said. And Dimitrios, two days home, had been seen to grin a little. Pethi guessed the Mayor wanted to say thank you, officially, for what they had done for Serifos.

But now they understood. The meeting place, the little square which opened at one side on to the blue harbour, was transformed.

Four immensely long tables filled it. They were covered in sun-dazzling white cloths, heaped and smothered with food. Fresh bread, fruit, cheeses, olives, salt fish, and jugs of wine. Leaves and flowers garlanded the plates and glasses. And swinging above it all, across the far end of the square, was a huge banner with painted blue letters. It said:.

THANK YOU

PETHI, VLEPPO, TINI

from all the Serifiots

'How embarrassing,' Tini muttered again, stepping backwards.

Nobody was about. Rows of chairs and benches waited, empty.

'Embarrassing?' Pethi astounded her by appearing far more pleased than uncomfortable. 'Why?'

She writhed. 'Well . . . ' waving a hand, 'all this, for us.' She backed away again.

'It's thanks. What's embarrassing about being thanked for something?'

There was no reply to this graceful logic. Pethi's dark eyes and Vleppo's gold ones looked at her frankly. Tini cast about in her mind to explain her discomfort.

'Well . . . ' she began again. 'Look at me. In my old jeans. Dad didn't say . . . And you! Look at you.'

Pethi laughed. 'What's that got to do with it?'

There was no reply to that either, and no time for one, for the square erupted.

People burst from doorways, sprang from low windows. At the same time upper windows were flung open, and flowers rained on the square. Everybody was calling their names. Out of a taverna swung two musicians, a fiddler and a bouzouki player. Behind them came, beamingly, George, Jason and Zoë, Dimitrios and Aspassia, and a host of villagers and friends. From another door walked the village Mayor with plump dignity.

They were surrounded by people shouting, cheering, hugging, stroking and kissing them. If Tini had hoped to escape it was now impossible. The Mayor bowed, took their hands, and led them to their seats, one at the head of each of the centre tables.

Tini sat, quivering. Any minute, she feared, she would cry.

She fought with an awful twitch in her chin, glancing across at Pethi. He sat straight, smiling, with Vleppo beside him, accepting the adulation with tremendous poise. As for the tears in his eyes, he wasn't in the least ashamed of them. She envied him.

Hot-faced she turned back to her table, now filling with village friends led by Zoë. And George. She gave him a wild-eyed look and hissed, 'Why didn't you tell me, rat?'

He poured her some wine, blandly. 'You would've gone in the other direction. And everyone wants to thank you.' George looked round the thronged square. 'Don't you know what you've done?' Tini said nothing. George pushed a wineglass into her hand. 'Drink that. You'll feel better.'

Noise rang round the square. Chairs and benches filled, plates were passed up and down, the choicest portions were selected – with shouted instructions – for the heroes. Music squeaked and lilted through the laughter and talk. The *panigiri*, the celebration, had begun.

'Pethi,' the tall *pappas* bent over him, pushing between Aspassia and Dimitrios. 'What a *fasaria* you've caused.' He was laughing, shaking Dimitrios' hand. 'Back already?' he teased him. Aspassia was wagging her head and waving her arms to indicate the load of trouble she had with her husband home again.

'A month, a month away!' Dimitrios protested. 'Soon, I am back at work.'

'Ach, he is a foolish man.' Aspassia loaded Dimitrios' plate with wholesome food.

'A month,' Pethi said. 'It doesn't seem so long ago. But look what's happened since . . . '

173

'Yes,' the *pappas* nodded, gazing round the square. Joyful islanders' faces. Then he looked down at Pethi, collecting a thought for words, but only said 'Yes,' again and smiled, touched the boy's shoulder, and moved away. Pethi watched him bend his long back to speak to Tini, who at once insisted he sit next to her. George was moved along a place unceremoniously.

They were a handsome contrast, Tini's bright face and the straight-nosed bearded one. Pethi remembered Tini saying that the *pappas* appeared to understand a lot without being told. Nevertheless, she was telling him something now, animatedly, pouring wine into his glass. Pethi grinned. She felt better, that was obvious.

'A good man is our *pappas*,' Aspassia shrieked in his ear, slapping his arm vigorously.

A cheer rose. Into the square came a troupe of village women, carrying hot dishes from the village ovens. The olives, cheese, and cold things were eaten. Now was the time for real feasting. *Moussakas* and stuffed peppers, chicken steaming in wondrous juices, baked fish running with lemon and olive oil. Such a day for Serifos.

Dimitrios heaped Pethi's plate. 'You will need strength,' he insisted, 'if you are to dig, and learn to be an archaeologist like the Sir Rolf.' Everyone was proud of Pethi's wish, at last admitted, to keep studying, perhaps to go to the University in Athens. It was an ambition he had always buried. University was a rare thing for a Serifiot: such ideas cost a great deal of money. So, he would be a fisherman. But now, Serifos would have some money, and Pethi could earn.

'I shall fish too,' Pethi replied. He could never give up the sea.

'Naturally!' Dimitrios flashed his grin. 'That is the most important thing. And you will need even more strength for that.'

Pethi grinned back in happiness. It was too much joy for expression, seeing his friend back again on the island. Perhaps a little thinner, possibly a shade paler. But in any way that mattered, the same.

The tables were debris and leaning elbows. Wine and water were leisurely sipped. Everyone relaxed, marvellously replete. The shouting and calling were now reduced to a general babble of conversation, of stories being told over again. Spiros and Aspassia, for perhaps the fiftieth time, were telling Dimitrios the drama of Thanos' madness. And how he had flown into another fury when word had come of Dimitrios' disappearance. And his rapid departure after warning had reached him from Athens. Nobody knew where he had gone, least of all the wretched Damia. The only feeling of unease left in the island: Thanos was not yet caught.

'Ach!' Aspassia cried. 'That Thanos, he should be rotting in jail!' She banged the wine jug on the table.

'What difference?' Spiros was philosophical. 'As long as he took no treasures, as we hope, and as long as he doesn't return. The island, remember, has his house.'

Pethi looked at Dimitrios. 'The island?'

Dimitrios nodded. 'Of course. It will be our museum, eh? A good idea. For the treasures that George and the Sir Rolf will dig up from the ground. It will make a beautiful museum.'

'What if they don't find much.' Pethi grinned. 'It'll be a big museum for only one head, one hand, and a shield.'

'*Po, po, po, po, po,*' cried Aspassia, 'you torment us Pethi.

That house will be filled in every room. And Thanos, may his dreams be black.' She devoured some cheese with relish.

Spiros quaffed his wine. 'See, Pethi – ' he indicated people along the table, ' – already the island is full again.'

One of the happy groups in the square was of three families whose men had returned to the island only yesterday, from Athens. Now they could work here, in the mines or the dig. It was for this, Pethi knew, more than for any glory of ancient finds, that the Serifiots were thanking them. Now the wives hung round their husbands' necks, children climbed on knees, life was good. The goddess had done this.

With a shout, Spiros sprang to his feet. In a bound he was in front of the musicians. A space cleared on the flagstones as Spiros raised his wineglass to the bouzouki player, then the fiddler. They swung into a new tune, with an understanding smile. To a run of metallic notes, Spiros put his glass on the ground. And then he danced.

Alone he swayed, this small, muscular island miner. He leaned, swooped, and leapt. He danced with a remote but strangely peaceful expression: he danced for himself, and the joy he felt. This dance wasn't meant as a spectacle. If anyone wished to watch, let them, but it wasn't important. At the end, nobody would applaud. It was the *zembékika*, the dance of deep emotions, danced alone. Spiros danced for his island and his own happiness. Pethi could almost have danced too.

As Spiros bent and twisted through the last slow movements, lifting his wineglass from the ground in his mouth to drain the last drop, others rose and joined in small groups for different dances. Now handkerchiefs whirled, heels were slapped, skirts lifted. The square vibrated.

Pethi saw, at the next table, Zoë and George in deep conversation. George was waving his hands, like any Greek. Zoë looked happy. It occurred to Pethi that he had never thought before of whether or not his mother was happy.

Tini's silvery head was still inclined towards the tall black hat of the *pappas*. What would have happened, Pethi thought, if she and George hadn't come to Serifos? It was they who should get all the thanks. He rested a hand on Vleppo's smooth back. If they hadn't come, with their ideas and curiosity, Thanos would have won. He would have deprived the island of its menfolk and let it die. And the cave, the goddess, the mystery . . . they would be secrets still, but useless ones, for Pethi himself, and Vleppo. Or worse, found by Thanos and lost to the island for ever.

The cave. It was a sudden, urgent compulsion. They must go back to the cave. To say some kind of farewell, perhaps. At first, because of that terrifying evening, they hadn't wanted to go. Then came people from Athens, crawling all over it, searching, exploring, taking out the sculptures. But now . . . Pethi tried to catch Tini's attention, but she was absorbed in talk. He was on the point of rising, but in that moment the Mayor himself stood, portly, smiling and flushed, lifting his hands for silence.

It was a silence interrupted by cheers as the Mayor thanked Pethi and Tini, with a special word for Vleppo. He called them 'fine, brave Serifiots', and referred to Zoë as a 'true Greek mother', which made her laugh behind her hand. George was complimented, and of course Dimitrios. Then the Mayor's friendly tone changed to one of black melodrama as he spoke of the fiendish attack arranged by Thanos for his own brother; the gathering was treated to a list of words describing Thanos with increasing distaste. Dimitrios looked embarrassed. Waving his plump hands, smoothing his moustache, the Mayor declaimed Thanos' wicked deeds. It was disgraceful indeed, and incredible, he said, that this man had got away with so much, among them all, for so long. He paused to draw breath.

And a man's voice broke into the short silence. It was one of the men just returned from Athens.

'Eh, Mr Mayor,' he called sarcastically. 'Of course you suspected nothing of it, hey, while it happened? No, no, you were not in fear of Thanos. *You* would never have hesitated to expose him!'

A few people laughed and cheered in a general rustle of interest. The Mayor turned dark red. So did the policeman. Fear of Thanos, and his Athens connections, had made any authority turn its back. There was a fidgety silence. Then Zoë's voice came, not loudly, but clear.

'Every Serifiot feared Thanos,' she said. 'All of us could have done something, if we had done it together.'

It was enough, and truthful. There was a pause, then a shout of approval. The islanders forgave their well-meaning Mayor and policeman. They crowded to pat their backs and say they had done their best, surely, for who would not have done the same things, in their shoes? Wine flowed again, and with it, the music.

But within seconds, a shock.

One of the women, turning to join a dance, glanced casually out towards the sunny harbour. And screamed.

'He returns!' Everyone froze. 'Look, look – Thanos – he is coming back!'

The music, the party died. Chairs fell as people leapt up to gather and stare.

Thanos' big white launch. It was just in the harbour, clear and bright, cutting the calm water in an arching spray, heading for the pier. In the sudden quiet the engine was a menacing roar through the hot afternoon. It was hideously unbelievable.

Tini was at Pethi's shoulder. 'He can't. He *can't*,' she whispered. Then was pushed aside by the Mayor and the policeman, who thrust through the incredulous crowd to the front. This time, after their first moment of horror, they were not going to fear Thanos. The islanders could rely on them. Firmly, side by side, the two marched out of the square on to the quay, to turn and stride towards the pier. The launch curved nearer.

The villagers watched them for a few silent seconds, and then, in a body, they followed. Everybody walked down the quay, a dense, soberly determined throng. The smiles had gone. Pethi, with Vleppo clinging on his shoulders, ran round the edge of the crowd, pulling Tini by the wrist.

The launch had slowed, but still it came closer. The plump Mayor and the young policeman led the crowd. Silent, waiting, the villagers stopped at the beginning of the pier. The boat's engine was the only sound. Without hesitating, it glided nearer, nearer.

Then Pethi stared. Surely – ? He glanced at the Mayor, the policeman. Had they seen? Then he looked at the launch again. Yes. On board a man was waving. Waving!

'Eh!' said the Mayor sharply. 'What is this?'

It was unbelievable. The village was dumbfounded. Could even Thanos have so much presumptuousness? Had he gone truly mad?

Then – 'That's not Thanos!' cried Tini.

'It's the police!' Pethi realized.

Then everyone was shouting, pushing forward. The launch was moored. Three policemen struggled on to the pier and into the crowd. And in the midst of the shouts, the questions, the shoving, the disbelief, the story came out.

These police were from the island of Lesvos, very near the Turkish coast. One of them, early yesterday morning in his garden, had heard a boat's engine. His house was by a quiet inlet; few people came there. Curiously, he looked. And saw Thanos' launch sneak in to moor. Like all the island police he knew the story of Serifos and was alert. He watched. Men on board came furtively ashore, seemed to be buying supplies. He waited. And last night, the police had arrested Thanos on his boat.

Thanos had been hiding out in Turkey with contacts there. Organizing his money, arranging some deal. One of the frightened men arrested with him revealed that Thanos now planned a night trip back to Serifos, to collect his woman and other things, 'before those stupid islanders could find what was his.' The same man told of a box, a locked chest. The police found it on the launch. Inside, the excited policeman told, were hundreds of silver coins, yes, centuries old, with the head of the goddess Athene on one side, and her little owl on the other. And an ancient silver cup, all engraved with pictures from some old myth about Medusa.

Tini and Pethi felt their minds reel to hear it. The goddess' own coins, ancient, priceless. And a silver cup . . . Thanos would have taken them away, far away. But now they were being carried safely to Athens, with Thanos, in a police launch. And the triumphant Lesvos police had brought Thanos' boat and the news to Serifos.

Suddenly the villagers were cheering and laughing. If there was happiness before, now it was enhanced by relief. Thanos was truly gone. The last shred of unease vanished, everyone was congratulating the smiling visitors.

The end of the story, Pethi thought. Or . . . not quite. He turned to see Tini's brilliant blue eyes on him. She nodded as his eyebrows lifted, and only Zoë noticed as they slid away from the noisy crowd.

The village returned to its party, taking the heroes from Lesvos with them. The music had begun again before they reached the square.

'Are we going in the *Petros*?'

Pethi nodded. 'It's easier that way, especially as they widened the ledge when they explored the cave and took everything out. So George said.' He glanced at Tini. 'How did you know we were going to the cave?'

'Haven't you learned not to ask questions like that?' she laughed. 'I just knew.'

They walked through the shimmering heat to the jetty.

Tini added, 'It was time somehow. Now the goddess has gone . . . we had to go back, sometime.'

The marble head of Athene, with her curved hand and lovely shield, were in the Mayor's offices. They had seen her, propped on a shelf, pensive, lost. In her presence now, away from her mysterious cave, they could sense none of the inexplicable power that had so affected the lives of everyone on the island.

'She's waiting for her temple,' Pethi had said.

Next week, perhaps, when the first team of archaeologists arrived, they might find the very site of that temple. The tape-recording had given remarkable directions, using names of places from ancient times. Weeks had passed in deciphering them, using old maps and museum documents. George was almost sure now of the place, he said.

Nothing more had been found in the cave. Experts had searched every cleft and crevice. They found that the chimney was almost blocked at the top where it emerged on the clifftop. Rocks, probably disturbed when Vleppo had climbed out, had fallen into the mouth. The men had cleared them easily enough, but it explained why Vleppo had come back by way of the cliffs on that dreadful evening.

'Sir Rolf said yesterday,' Pethi remembered as they glided out of the harbour under red sails, 'that he thinks the statue was lowered into the cave down the chimney, by people who wanted to hide her. And it broke. And possibly other people, later, took away pieces, only this time by the cliffs probably, and by sea.'

'Maybe those people were the thieves, like the voice said, dashed from the cliffs. Horrible.'

A diving party would be among the archaeologists: it was more than likely, Sir Rolf had said, that some treasures were on the sea bed. Especially as George's translation of the last part of the recording had revealed some confused ramblings about caverns of the sea, and grumbling comments that Poseidon, god of the oceans and the earth, couldn't be trusted to guard Athene's valuable property.

'Suppose they find all of her,' Tini imagined. 'To stand in her temple. In a long robe, and helmet, with her shield and spear and owl.'

'And the rest of her silver treasures all about her.'

The wide-eyed goddess stood clearly in their minds as the *Petros* smacked over the bright waves, leaning elegantly, tossing foam behind.

The wind flung Tini's hair in shining streamers as the boat flew. Pethi looked at her.

'D'you know what they're calling you? The fishermen?'

'What? What do you mean?' She turned, her vivid eyes puzzled.

Pethi grinned. 'Little goddess.'

'Oh, for heaven's sake.' It came out in English, cross and embarrassed.

He laughed. 'Oh, for heaven's sake!' he imitated. 'That's a suitable reply in the circumstances.' She scowled at him as he rocked.

They were in the bay at last. The wind dropped, the sea smoothed. There, high above in the reddish cliff face, their cave.

'Tini?' Pethi was turned away, long thin arms pulling at the sails.

'Hm?'

'Do you suppose you'd have time to teach me some English?' It was unbelievably casual.

Tini looked at Pethi, his expression all concentration on his boat. His hair windblown and wild, a dark eyebrow lifted to sneak her a glance as he dropped anchor. 'Well?' he said.

'What, me?' She couldn't resist it. 'A girl?'

He leaned towards her, all innocence, and kissed her cheek. 'A girl?' he said surprised. 'But surely the fishermen say – '

With a heave, she pushed him over the side into the clear water.

15

Everything was different. As soon as they reached the stalactite cavern they knew. Even here now, daylight stretched pale fingers where the entrance led to the goddess' cave. The chimney had been opened and widened by the searchers: once, they said, at the time the statue had been lowered into the cave, the entrance may well have been this wide. But centuries of earth tremor and falling rock had closed it in.

Pethi and Tini walked slowly through to the mysterious cave of the goddess. Almost fearfully.

Now the light was quite strong, compared with the diffused and pearly twilight they had known. The cave had new colours, new outlines. Boldness and cheerfulness instead of subtlety and mystery.

'Gone,' said Tini.

'The feeling. Yes.' Pethi couldn't recapture the sense of magical power. It had left the cave, vanished.

'But there's still something. Different though.'

They sat beneath the bright chimney, leaning back on the smooth rock floor, staring upwards.

'Peaceful. Yes, it's peaceful,' Pethi murmured.

'As if . . . '

'What?'

'As if there's a problem finally solved. Something like that.'

'I feel that. And it's like – well, happiness being here. In the air of the cave. But that sounds stupid.'

'It doesn't.'

They sat in the peacefulness. Quiet. Vleppo curled beside Pethi as if he had no further interest in the place.

'I told the *pappas*,' Tini said. 'All of it. How we felt here, and everything that happened.'

'I thought so.' Pethi looked at her fair, serious face and considered again how Tini had altered all his life.

'He just . . . accepted it all. Without question. He understood somehow. He wasn't even surprised, not in the least.'

'As you'd said.'

'Even then, I couldn't help expecting a priest to try and make me see it in his terms. In fact, I would almost have welcomed it – some kind of explanation. But he didn't even try it. He said religions in Greece have become all mixed together, since before the time of the ancient gods on Mount Olympus. And onwards, for ever, he said. And maybe that was the best way to have religions and myths. Mixed, and growing. Continuing. He said maybe one shouldn't look for quick and easy answers because they turn into rules. I couldn't follow it all.'

'No. But I expect he's right. Though it doesn't explain anything – the cave, the feelings, the voice . . . ' Pethi saw that they would never know.

'He said, acceptance, not explanations. I'm going to have to think about that.'

They were silent again for a while. Then Pethi said:

'And the cats?' He grinned.

'From mysticism to cats . . . ' glancing at the sleeping

Vleppo, 'but maybe that's not so odd. Yes, I'm going to help with the *pappas*' cat schemes. He's got some good ideas. We'll set up a kind of cat veterinary surgery.' She laughed. 'Everyone will think me mad.'

At that moment Vleppo awoke with a peremptory yowl, standing and stretching with arched back. His extra toes spread, and retracted. He looked round the cave with an air of finality, his moon eyes glowing in his fine black face. As if he had been given some signal to leave.

Automatically Pethi and Tini got up from the floor and followed Vleppo slowly across the cave.

'He knows she's gone,' Tini said. 'It's all gone.'

'Maybe, when they find the temple . . . ' Pethi murmured.

'Maybe.'

They stopped at the archway into the big cavern.

'That's it then,' Pethi said pointlessly. They stood looking back across the light-bathed rock floor. Empty. 'See you in your temple, Athene.'

They both jumped as the sharpness of the little owl's screech sounded down the chimney. Once, twice. And faintly, faintly, the soft flurry of wings. Rising, leaving.

Then, as they waited, there floated down on a current of air and the silvery light, down to the floor of the cave, a feather. They watched it land where the marble head of the goddess had lain.

Author's Note

As the map of Greece shows, Serifos exists.

It was on this island's rocky shore, says the myth, that Danaë, the moon-goddess, was left by the waves, with her tiny baby Perseus.

Danaë, young and beautiful, had been turned out of her home by her father Acrisius, king of Argos.

The trouble began when Acrisius was told by the Oracle that his grandson would grow up to kill him. He tried to defeat the prophecy by keeping his daughter Danaë under lock and key, away from her uncle (the king's own brother) who had a passion for the girl.

But lock and key don't keep out a god. Zeus, greatest of the gods, had fallen in love with Danaë. He turned himself into a shower of gold and entered her room, and made love to her. When, as a result, she gave birth to a son, her father in terror locked her and the baby into a wooden ark and cast them into the sea.

The ark was found, washed up on Serifos, by one Dictys. Dictys was a fisherman, and brother of the king of Serifos, Polydictys. (Some versions of the myth say that they were brother-kings.) Polydictys, the elder brother, wanted to marry Danaë, but she resisted him. As her son Perseus grew up, the king resented him, seeing him as the obstacle to his wishes.

Eventually Polydictys, who was undoubtedly cunning, put about the rumour that he planned to marry a princess, one Hippodameia, and that the young men of Serifos should pay their respects with gifts and money.

Perseus, glad that Polydictys would now stop pestering his mother, wanted to bring the royal couple a fine gift, but had nothing. So, just as Polydictys slyly hoped, the brave youth offered to get him anything he should ask in the world. At once the king demanded the head of the Medusa, a terrible female being with hideous face and hair of snakes. To look upon her meant to be turned to stone. Perseus agreed at once, to Polydictys' delight. He was sure he had guaranteed the death of the young man, and could win Danaë without further trouble.

But Perseus had a friend in the flashing-eyed goddess Athene. She gave him a brilliant shield and, through her half-brother Hermes, winged sandals, a magical sickle, a helmet of invisibility, and a bag for the Medusa's head.

After many adventures Perseus arrived at the Medusa's lair and sliced off her head without looking directly at her – using the shield of Athene as a mirror. He flew back on winged feet to Serifos, enjoying more excitements on the way, including rescuing the fair Andromeda from a Monster and marrying her.

On Serifos his mother Danaë was in hiding from the king Polydictys whose attentions had become alarming. The king himself was in his palace with his cronies, planning more dark deeds, and was astounded to see Perseus stride in.

The announcement that he had brought the requested gift drew mocking laughter and shouts of disbelief from the company, so Perseus opened his bag and pulled out the gruesome be-snaked head, keeping his own face turned away. At once all the men, including Polydictys, were turned to stone where they stood.

The king's brother Dictys, who had helped Danaë in her flight, was of course spared. However, several other enemies were turned to stone, as well as some unfortunate stray animals. The frogs of the island, the story goes, were struck dumb with fright. All of which explains the circle of stones, or ring of mountains, which forms the island of Serifos. These are the petrified enemies of Perseus, Athene and Danaë.

Finally Perseus gave the Medusa's head to the goddess Athene, who fixed it to her shield, where it remained always.

Perseus, it turned out, did as the Oracle had forecast and eventually (unwittingly) caused the death of his own grandfather, but that is part of another story.

If you go to Serifos today you will not necessarily find every person and thing in this book. Many have been invented, many are typical of Greek islands generally. But the myth really was based on Serifos, and Greek myths are for ever.

Nobody has actually found a statue of Athene on the island, or, indeed, her temple. But nobody, as far as is known, has looked.